BETWEEN ICE AND OATHS

CRIMSON ICE
BOOK 2

WILLOW FOX

SLOW BURN PUBLISHING

ONE

HARPER

Dante retrieves a file that has been sitting on his lap, hidden beneath the table. He opens the folder, the contents staring me straight in the face.

The air rushes out of my lungs as I stare at the birth certificate.

No one was supposed to know.

"You failed to mention that you have a son."

I glance at Luca. This isn't how I wanted him to find out. I had planned on telling him when things got serious between us.

We jumped from planning our first real date to an engagement overnight. That somehow is entirely my fault. I thought I heard a whimpering puppy and followed the sound in the middle of the night.

Turns out, I was wrong.

It wasn't an animal, but a little boy all of eight years old, being held prisoner in the Ricci's basement.

From there, I made the near-deadly mistake of trying to help the little one flee on foot, which only got us both dragged back down to the dungeon and nearly killed.

Dante, Luca's father, offered me one way out, to shoot one of his men who had betrayed him.

I'm not a murderer.

I could never hurt anyone, unless perhaps it were in self-defense, or I suppose if anyone laid a hand on *my* son.

A mother's fury is undeniable.

Dante wanted me dead. Ordered my execution. That was last night.

Of course, Luca stepped in, my proverbial knight in shining armor, in sweats and a t-shirt, insisting that we marry, he would work for his father, and I would be protected by the family.

It still doesn't sit well with me, the idea of marrying for protection instead of love, and marrying into *this* family, filled with monsters and murderers.

But my life is on the line, as is Luca's.

I heard the order, that Ashton Rinaldi was tasked with executing both Luca and me if we don't follow orders.

Can't say I'm disappointed that Ashton isn't sitting at this dinner table tonight. He left early and returned to Evergreen University.

Wish I could have gone back to campus, too, but instead, I'm forced to face Luca's parents in the flesh and Nova's parents, because they happen to work closely with the Riccis.

It's like a family reunion, and I'm being served as the meal.

Luca's eyes tighten, and I can see the pain that I've caused. His gray eyes swirl like a December sky, heavy with clouds, turbulent winds blowing in and a winter storm brewing.

"You have a son?" he seethes, shock evident on his face.

The birth certificate—a reminder of the little boy I love desperately, who I'd do anything to protect.

I knew this day would come. I just thought I would be the one explaining to Luca about my son.

He deserves to hear the truth from me.

"I do," I say and nod slowly. Admitting the truth is the only way through this, with all eyes on me, like I'm the villain in this story.

Meanwhile, I'm seated at a table with actual criminals, men who live and breathe for the mafia.

"His name is Zeke," I say. My heart floods with warmth just thinking about my son. I love him more than anything, anyone. It pains me to be apart from him right now.

"Did you give him up for adoption?" Luca asks.

It's a fair question. I've never mentioned Zeke to

Luca or to anyone at Evergreen. Not even my best friend, Kensley, knows about my son.

While I live on campus because of my scholarship, I had to choose between my education and raising my son at home with my parents and getting a job straight out of high school.

The decision was made for me.

Just like every decision since I got pregnant. I have to put my son first, my family first, and myself a solid second or even third.

"No, he lives with my parents," I say.

Luca pushes his chair from the table and gets up, walking away in a huff.

"Luca!" I call after him.

"Let him go," Dante growls. "We're not done."

I hate watching him walk off, even more so knowing that he's hurting and I'm the reason for his pain.

I did intend to tell him, but it's not a conversation that just comes up when you're studying together, as friends.

Our relationship has barely scratched the surface.

I have to let Luca walk off the anger. What other choice do I have right now?

If I could wish him to come back, sit down, listen as I explain everything, it would be so much easier. But his footsteps disappear over the marble flooring, and I no longer can hear him in the distance.

"What do you want to know?" I ask, turning my attention back to Luca's father, staring at Dante pointedly.

Since he dug up my past, there must be some reason he decided to expose it.

"For starters, when were you going to tell us you have a child?" Nikki asks. "You're intending to marry my son; did you not think this is important information that, at the very least, he should have?" Her voice rises, and I recognize why she's upset.

But the engagement wasn't born out of love; it was out of need and survival.

"Zeke doesn't live with me."

"Obviously," Dante says, rolling his eyes. "You live on campus. We've established that Zeke lives with your parents. Does he believe them to be his parents? Did you relinquish your parental rights to your parents?"

It's a lot of questions, and I reach for my water glass, feeling parched.

"My parents are helping me raise Zeke."

"Seems more like they're raising him for you," Dante quips.

It's a gut punch, and I take it, because maybe I do deserve it. Every day that I'm not with Zeke, I feel guilty.

"My education is important to both of my parents. They want me to be able to take care of Zeke on my own after I graduate."

"So, his biological father isn't in the picture?" Nikki asks. "The birth certificate didn't list a father."

"*He* relinquished his paternal rights," I say. "He has no involvement with Zeke and never will."

Dante and Nikki exchange a glance. I'm not sure what they're thinking.

The table is momentarily quiet. Moreno and Paige sit farther away, and Nova is seated next to me, but apparently, I've left her speechless as well. I'm glad Moreno isn't butting in, but at the same time, I feel like I'm left alone to defend my actions, which happen to be none of their business.

Nova reaches for my arm, resting a hand on it. Her gesture is comforting, but it's not nearly enough with the interrogation going on right now with Luca's parents.

Dante glances at the birth certificate. "Based on his date of birth, your son is little more than a toddler."

"He's two," I say, staring at them.

"What kind of a mother leaves her child and goes off to school for four years?" Dante's question is cold, and I can't help but know how it looks.

"My scholarship requires me to live on campus. I tried to get an exemption and even requested to live on campus in one of the houses or apartments instead of the dorms, but I was denied because I filed too late and didn't have the additional funds to cover the added expenditures for the application."

That is on me, but I also hadn't known about the scholarship until the last minute. A secret my parents had kept from me while they were deciding my future.

"You live in the dorms; won't that be problematic once you and Luca are wed?" Nikki asks.

I take another sip of water and place the glass back down. "We haven't exactly discussed living arrangements. The engagement was just last night," I say and glance at Dante.

I'm not sure how much Nikki knows about what happened. Luca seems to believe she knows the entire story, but I'm not ready to divulge it if she doesn't.

"Given the requirements of your scholarship, we have secured a more suitable property for all of you to live in, which is still on campus. Beginning the first Monday in January, the house is yours. That includes a room for Nova," Nikki says, glancing at her, "as well as for Ashton and Liam."

"Thank you," Nova says, her eyes widening with delight. "We get to live together," she says, grinning at me.

I wish I were as excited, but knowing that Ashton

will be on the premises has me slightly concerned. After all, he was ordered to kill Luca and me.

"And it won't affect my scholarship?" I ask, needing to know that my education will continue. I don't have the funds to pay for four years of college.

"It is considered on-campus housing. You're not the only one on a scholarship," Nikki says. "As for the additional expenditures, Dante and I will handle those costs, as we do for our son, we will do for our newly appointed daughter."

Dante glares at Nikki, displeased, but he doesn't argue aloud.

"Thank you, that's quite generous of you," I say.

While I don't intend to accept their money, knowing the arrangements have already been made is a huge relief.

I'll get to have Zeke with me soon.

"And the wedding, are you still requiring that we remain here until that happens?" It's a heavy ask, considering Luca and I have school on Monday. I can't miss my classes. I need to keep my grades up to retain my scholarship.

I'll also need to find time to get a part-time job while raising Zeke to cover any additional expenses, which is going to cut into my studying.

Overwhelmed is an understatement, but at least I feel slightly hopeful. I hadn't wanted to live in the dorms.

While Nikki might be offering to help cover a few dollars in regard to the housing expenses, which I won't let her do, I will gratefully accept the opportunity to move out of the dorms, away from Quinn.

But I won't owe Nikki or Dante.

Not now. Not ever.

Dante and Nikki share a brief glance, and then she leans in, whispering something to him. I'm hoping that she's on my side. I spent time with her, we went to lunch, maybe she can talk reason into her husband.

Nikki pulls back briefly, and Dante glowers at me.

"We trust that you won't tell anyone our family secret, because it would put your family, including your son, Zeke, in danger. You wouldn't want to hurt everyone you care about, would you?" Dante threatens.

"Of course, she wouldn't," Nikki says. "She's a smart girl. She knows family comes first. With that said, since we can procure a place outside of the dorms, will Zeke be living with you, or will he remain with your parents?"

Dante glances at Nikki. "Perhaps that is something she should discuss with Luca first."

"Please," I say, glancing back over my shoulder in the direction he disappeared. I want to talk to him and explain everything.

Will he forgive me?

And if he doesn't, what does that mean for the marriage?

Will his parents have me and my family killed if we don't wed?

"After dinner," Dante says as the food is brought to the table.

I glance at the empty chair beside me.

Does Luca intend on skipping dinner?

I wouldn't blame him for it. If I had the opportunity, I'd rather be stashed away someplace else.

Then again, if it were me, I'd have hightailed it out of here with the car. Luca had planned on driving me back to campus, but now, I don't know what plans await us.

Nova nudges me as she grabs a dinner roll. "Don't worry, Luca will be fine."

He'll be fine. I'm just not sure that he'll forgive me.

———

Dinner is contentious, and I'm relieved when I can finally get up from the table without being rude or scolded by his father.

"Do you want me to find Luca for you?" Nova asks as she gets up from the dinner table.

"That would be appreciated." I don't want to wander aimlessly around the house. The last time I did that, it ended with me in this predicament, forced to marry Luca.

Which wouldn't be terrible if we'd have been dating for a couple of years.

We were just scratching the surface, turning a budding friendship into something a little more heated.

Now, I worry the heat will be directed entirely at me, but not in romantic gestures as much as being scorched with his anger.

I hear the two of them before I see them round the corner.

Luca's eyes are steel. His expression fueled with anger as he carries his bag and mine.

"Let's go," he says and heads for the back door where our coat and shoes await us.

I don't bother with pleasantries with his family. What's the point? I slip into my heels that I foolishly brought with me, and slide my coat on, buttoning it.

"Bye," he shouts over his shoulder.

Nikki comes hurrying into the hallway, pulling her son into a hug. She gives me one too, but it's a little more forced. "I'll see you next weekend, Luca," she says.

"Yeah," Luca mutters, tossing the door open and waltzing outside.

I hurry after him, two steps behind. Between his long strides and my heels, I am definitely not capable of keeping up.

He doesn't bother offering me an arm to help steady me. The ground is soft from the recent thaw of snow, and my heel catches in the ground, knocking me off balance.

I fall, landing on him, knocking us both down to the ground.

He curses as he face plants into the grass without warning.

"I'm sorry." I'm quick to apologize, but I don't think it will help. I'm half on top of him and slink my way back as he climbs onto his knees and then stands.

I'm only half-covered in dirt and grass, while Luca is a bit messier. But he offers me his hand, helping me regain my footing.

Once I'm recovered, standing firmly on the grass, he dusts off the dirt. He's lucky he's not caked in mud. There are grass stains, but they brandish his coat and his knees, clad in jeans.

"Be careful," he says and grabs my arm, helping me the remainder of the way to the car.

I get the distinct feeling that he's helping me so that I don't trample him a second time.

As we approach his vehicle out front, he unlocks the car and tosses our bags into the backseat before climbing into the driver's side.

I slink into the passenger seat in the front, shut the door, and wait for him to scream at me.

But he doesn't say anything.

At least not yet.

The silence is even worse.

The air is thick with tension, and while it's chilly outside, the car feels a hundred degrees. I buckle my seatbelt, and he turns off the radio, driving us up to the wrought iron gates.

We wait for the guard to allow us to leave.

Slowly, they open the entrance and Luca slams on the gas, tearing out of the driveway in haste.

I'm silent. I don't know what to say to fix the damage that's been done.

I can hear each breath he takes. They're long, pronounced, and filled with a sigh, like he's inwardly fighting with himself.

After several minutes, I finally gather the courage to say something. "Can I explain?" My voice falters as I shift in my seat.

His grip tightens on the steering wheel, his jaw tense as he doesn't so much as look at me.

"Explain how you lied to me. Sure, go ahead." His tone is clipped, his anger edging its way out.

I deserve the wrath he's waiting to set upon me. I can feel it coming, ready to be unleashed.

"When I was in high school, I got pregnant."

His gaze flickers. "Boyfriend or—" He doesn't even want to say the word.

"Yes, he was a senior on the high school varsity football team," I say, as if that explains why I hate sports and avoid jocks.

"You slept with him and got knocked up. Got it."

It's much more complicated than that, but he's right, that is what happened. I expel a soft sigh and tilt my head back, staring up at the car ceiling.

"You can hate me all you want, Luca. You don't even have to marry me, but I just, I need to know that Zeke will be safe."

He runs a hand through his hair, frustrated, and then slams his hand on the steering wheel.

"Fuck!"

I glance at him, silent, watching him fall apart because of me.

"I'm sorry," I whisper.

"You don't get to apologize and think everything will be fixed." He shoots me daggers and then returns his focus to the road. Luca shifts in his seat and scratches his jaw. "Fuck."

"Maybe I can take Zeke and leave town for a while. I won't tell anyone why I'm leaving. Your family's secret will be safe."

He laughs darkly, and I feel the hair on my arms stand on end, like electricity humming through the air. "My father will never let you just run and disappear," Luca warns. "He has men everywhere."

"And you'll be one of them," I whisper, glancing down at my hands in my lap.

There's no engagement ring sitting on my finger. His mother discussed buying us wedding bands as a gift if we do go through with the marriage.

"Don't remind me what I'll be." Luca's voice is gruff, fueled with hatred. "I never wanted to work for Dante." He slams his hand on the steering wheel again, his anger boiling over.

"I'm sorry."

"There you go again, apologizing." He doesn't even glance at me, but maybe I should be grateful. It's better that he focuses on the road, getting us back to campus in one piece.

Silence fills the car once again.

Looking back, thinking about his reluctance for me to attend Nova's birthday party suddenly makes sense.

"This isn't all on me," I whisper, finding my strength as I glare at him. "If you told your father was mafia, I wouldn't have come."

"I tried warning you!" he shouts, and I feel a shiver course through me.

Suddenly, I'm no longer hot but ice cold. I reach for the vent and adjust the temperature on my side of the car, trying to get warm.

"Well, you should have tried harder," I mutter loud enough for him to hear me.

"You should have told me about Zeke!"

I glare at him. "When, Luca? When would have been a good time to tell you that I have a two-year-old son? That I'm a mom. That I already have my life planned out for me after college and that I'm struggling to get through the day because my child, who should need me, is being cared for by my parents."

"Any time before today," he seethes. "We had study dates together. You could have mentioned Zeke then. Or how about in class? You could have shown me a photo of your son on your phone. Hell, I put my phone number into your phone; he wasn't even a wallpaper on your screen. It's like you were trying to hide him."

"That's not fair." I shake my head, but maybe some small part of me believes him.

I did hide Zeke from everyone.

Kensley, my best friend at Evergreen, doesn't know about my son.

My shitty roommate, Quinn; I obviously wouldn't have told her.

He's a secret that I've been keeping, not to protect him, but to protect myself.

Because believing that I could have a normal college life was easier than facing the reality that I'm a teenage mom.

The worst part in all of it, was leaving him behind. "I didn't even want to come here," I say, staring out the side window.

"Then why the fuck did you come to Nova's birthday? I told you *not* to come."

He's angry with me. I'm not sure he'll ever forgive me.

"I wasn't talking about the party. I meant EU," I say.

He's silent. It's the first time in a while that I feel like he's letting me speak, or maybe he's just decided he doesn't care what I say, he's going to remain angry with me forever.

"That scholarship, Luca, it required me to live on campus. I wanted to commute so that I could go to college during the day, and then come home so I could be with Zeke as much as possible."

He shifts again but doesn't say anything.

I know he's listening, even when he pretends not to pay attention. His muscles flex and ripple as I speak. The tension bounds through him, unwilling to release.

"My parents decided for me that I would be coming here to get an education." They couldn't afford my tuition without the scholarship. It was an either or situation: attend full-time and live on campus, or live at home, get a job, and forgo the college degree.

"Don't blame this on your parents." Luca glares at me before returning his attention back on the road.

It's growing dark outside, and the drive back to campus isn't on heavily traveled roads.

"I take full responsibility for not telling you about Zeke," I say, making it clear I'm not blaming them. I was just trying to explain why he's not living with me and I'm in the dorms.

He huffs under his breath, ignoring me once again.

Silence fills the car. He reaches for the radio, deciding for himself that we're done talking.

As he pulls up to the quad and parks outside the dorms, he barely glances at me. He reaches into the backseat and retrieves my bag, handing it to me.

I step out of the vehicle, grab my bag from his hands, my fingers grazing his briefly. I stare at him, but he won't meet my gaze.

I guess we're not going on that date tomorrow if he won't even look at me, let alone speak to me. "Good luck at practice." I remember him telling his parents he had hockey practice tomorrow.

"See you in class," he says, and I feel like we've just broken up after a huge fight. Except we weren't dating.

We aren't technically anything, and yet we're engaged.

TWO

ASHTON

What a colossal fuck-up. What was supposed to be a get-together for Nova's birthday transpired into me getting orders to shoot my best friend and teammate, along with his *fake* girlfriend.

I lie back on the sofa, stretching out, drinking a beer.

I crave something to take my mind off what the hell went down this weekend. Thankfully, I was able to high-tail it out before their little family dinner.

I wanted zero involvement in the Ricci dinner dynamics. It doesn't take a genius to see that hell was going to be unleashed on Luca and Harper.

I actually like Luca. As a friend, he's great company and loyal, and as a roommate, he keeps his shit tidy. As a teammate, well, I know I can depend on him on the ice.

But having his father give me orders to kill my friend if Luca didn't kill Harper, well, that was some next-level fucked-up drama.

I'd have done it, because my old man, Aureilo, and Dante are friends, but I'm not thrilled about what was asked of me.

Luca should be home soon, assuming his father didn't murder him, no exaggeration.

I flip through the channels on our streaming app and nurse a beer.

It's Saturday night, getting late, but I should be out at a party, not replaying the night's events over in my head.

What a shitshow.

The front door squeaks open, and I glance over my shoulder.

Turns out Luca Ricci is still alive.

"I guess I'm not taking your position on the ice."

"Dark sarcasm, that's cute, but I'm not in the mood." Luca's voice reeks of annoyance and anger.

He's usually so levelheaded, except when it comes to Harper McKenna.

I sit up on the sofa, toss my legs over the side and glance at him, intrigued. "Your little engagement not going according to plan?" I smirk, knowing it'll piss him off. I can just feel the rage boiling off of him.

"No thanks to you," Luca growls at me and tosses his duffel bag on the floor. He drops his coat and shoes with it.

He's usually a bit tidier, but I just take another drink from my beer bottle and watch him cautiously. "Dinner went well, I take it."

He flips me off and storms into the kitchen, hitting the light switch on the wall. He opens and shuts the fridge repeatedly before banging around with the pots and pans.

It's giving me a headache.

"What the hell is your problem?" I shout at him and get my ass up off the sofa.

Fuck. I was just getting comfortable.

"You're my problem," Luca seethes and drops the metal pot onto the stove. "She's my problem."

He apparently has a list of who's wronged him.

Can't say I'm surprised that I've made the cut, especially after the shit that happened last night.

"Not marrying her?" I guess, a bit relieved. I'd hate to see him throw his life away for a girl he hardly knows. I can't help but smile as I sip my beer and watch his frustration get taken out on our cookware.

"You would like that, wouldn't you?" Luca growls and rushes at me. "You've been eyeing her all semester, vying for her attention."

While I did have a little crush on Harper when I first met her, I realized Luca had it *bad* for her, and his streak of jealousy wasn't going to help our friendship or the team.

Dad always taught me to put the team first, or maybe he'd actually meant the mafia, but I'm just using those words interchangeably. To me, they're both blood, family. Then again, I did hold a gun on Luca last night.

Not surprised he's pissed.

"Trust me, I'm not the one interested in marrying her," I say.

He laughs darkly.

"That's not what you said when you met her," he reminds me of my words, the ones where I swore I'd met the girl who I'd marry.

"Well, I was wrong. She clearly has eyes for you. I'm not going to compete with that," I say. If he's looking for a fight from me, I'm not giving it to him.

He drops a half-dozen ingredients into the pan, mostly veggies and some chicken, and watches the stove.

"What's gotten into you?" I ask.

"Seriously?" His gaze shoots up at me. "You were ready to follow my father's orders without so much as considering our brotherhood."

"Don't take it personal, my father and your dad are friends. I'm going to run the business one day, it's just—an order."

"Killing me is just a fucking order?" Luca shouts, his eyes wide, and I'm not sure he won't flip the pan at me. At least the food isn't sizzling hot yet. The pan, though, I'm not entirely sure. I take a step back.

I can see his father's rage in him.

"You'll make a good don," I say, hoping to ease the tension.

"I don't fucking want to be a don!" Luca grabs the nearest knife from the counter and throws it at me.

I duck just in time as it whizzes right past and slams into the wall. It would have taken out my eye or maybe my forehead. Not terrible aim.

"I don't think we're getting our safety deposit back," I joke, trying to make light of the situation.

Before I have time to hear his answer, I stalk backward out of the kitchen, not waiting for the second knife to strike.

"Asshole," I mutter.

"I heard that!" Luca shouts back at me.

"Good, it was meant for you to hear." I collapse back onto the sofa, trying to unwind, but it seems near impossible when my phone rings. I don't recognize the number, so I send the call to voicemail.

A second later, it buzzes with a text from the same unknown number.

It's Dante. Pick up the damn phone.

Why the hell is Luca's father calling and texting me? I glance at Luca, who is still preoccupied in the kitchen, and opt to take the call in my bedroom.

My cell phone rings again, and this time, I answer the call just as I step into my room, closing the door behind myself. "Yes, sir. What can I do for you?"

THREE

HARPER

I head to class and walk by Kensley on the way to Econ 101. We don't have any classes together this semester, but we spend lunch together almost every afternoon.

"You're not answering my texts," Kensley says with a playful glare in her eyes.

I reach into my pocket and glance at my phone. "You didn't send me anything." I show her my phone and the lack of text messages from her.

She snags it from my hands and pauses outside. She has to head east since we're going to different buildings. "Weird. Maybe reboot your phone."

It's been a while since I restarted my phone. "I'll try that," I say and shut it down, shoving it in my pocket in the meantime.

"Let's grab lunch later. Same time?" she asks, like I've been avoiding her, which I haven't.

Although I didn't text her this weekend, either. I was busy dealing with the aftermath of Nova's birthday party.

Sunday, I spent it lounging around, trying not to panic when I called my parents and didn't even gather enough strength to tell them I had a *fake* boyfriend, let alone a fiancé.

How am I going to tell Kensley I'm engaged?

She'll never buy it. She's been around me long enough to see that Luca and I aren't constantly all over each other.

A wedding would be absolutely insane.

"Of course, lunch later." I force a smile. I have so much that I want to tell her, but I'm not sure how. The last thing I want is to put her life in danger too.

I head through the heavy wooden doors and into the auditorium. There's no sign of Luca. Although he usually shows up after I get to class, choosing to sit next to me.

Something tells me he's going to choose a different seat today.

I sit in my usual spot, open my laptop, and grab my most recent notes, reviewing the lessons. Most of them make very little sense when I review them until Luca helps unjumble the information for me.

He's a good teacher.

And a really great friend.

But he doesn't show up for class. I grab my phone, turn it back on and send Luca a text.

Where are you?

It shows that he's read my message, but he doesn't respond.

He also doesn't show up for class. Is he avoiding me, or is something else wrong?

After class, I walk alone to my next lecture across campus. I hate to admit how lonely it feels without Luca walking with me. It always helped pass the time, and he is really good company.

At least class breezes by, and unlike economics where I completely suck, the English course is an easy A for me. After I finish, I swing by to grab lunch with Kensley and retrieve my phone from my bag.

There are still no messages from Luca. There also aren't any messages from Kensley, which is weird.

"I saved us a table," she says and waves to me. She's already grabbed a sandwich. I drop off my backpack and get in line to grab one too.

Ashton marches up behind me, making sure he hurries before anyone else takes the spot directly next to me. "Hey, stranger," he says with a smirk.

I size him up, unsure what the hell he's doing.

"Just grabbing lunch," he says, clearly recognizing my suspicion.

"Luca wasn't in class today. Everything okay?" I ask. I order a sandwich and wait for the girl behind the counter to prepare it for me.

"I don't know. He threw a knife at me the other day. Sunday, he didn't say a word to me during practice. Are you two doing okay?" Ashton asks.

I've never known him to inquire about Luca and me. After what transpired Saturday at the Ricci's home, I'm hesitant to share much. But he does know what's going on, and since I can't tell Kensley, maybe confiding in him is the next best option?

"I don't think so," I say. I grab a bag of chips and wait for Ashton to get his sandwich before we both head to the register to check out.

"Second guessing your choices?" Ashton asks.

I open my mouth but shut it. I'm not sure what he's saying, but I don't entirely trust him. Not after what happened over the weekend. "I guess you can say Luca and I aren't talking."

Ashton and I pay for our meals, and he walks with me to the table that Kensley is saving for us.

"Why aren't you and Luca talking?" Ashton asks, waiting for my answer.

He's definitely fishing for information. I'm just not sure why.

Is it out of mere curiosity or something more sinister?

I sit at the table, and he decides to join us, uninvited. "I'm Ashton," he says, putting down his tray and then holding out his hand to properly introduce himself.

Kensley is already munching down her sandwich and puts it down, then wipes her hands on her napkin before reaching for his hand. "Kensley," she says. "Sorry, you totally caught me off guard. Wasn't expecting new friends. But it's all good."

Kensley's eyes are wide, and she's trying to figure out what's going on.

"Kensley and I met the first week on campus," I say. "I know Ashton through Luca. They're roommates."

"You met me first," Ashton says, smirking.

He's wrong. I met Luca first, but Ashton technically asked me out first. I don't tell him that, it's not something he needs to know. Besides, it would probably just come back to bite me in the ass with Luca.

"Are you flirting with me?" I ask, trying to disarm whatever the hell he's up to.

Ashton quickly shifts uncomfortably in his seat. "No," he says and turns his attention to Kensley, like I just insulted him.

"So, how was your weekend?" Kensley asks. "You never called to tell me how that date with Luca went."

"It didn't happen," I say and glance down at my food, as though it were the most interesting thing in the world. I take a bite and hope Kensley won't ask anything more.

I'm not that lucky.

"Did hockey practice get in the way?" she asks.

"No, I did," I say and glance at Ashton.

Luca and I haven't spoken since Saturday night when he dropped me off back at school. "Luca is icing me out," I say.

Kensley frowns. "What'd you do?" she asks, leaning forward, completely engrossed in my lack of a love life.

Ashton watches me, and it's that look that says more than any words ever could. He's waiting to see if I break and reveal the truth about the Ricci family.

I won't. Besides, I don't even care that they're mafia. That's hardly news. The bigger story is that they've kidnapped a little boy, which I spent all day Sunday trying to figure out who the kid is, but I came up empty—until I saw the news on television.

An explosion had destroyed the home of a prominent businessman and his family, including, they believed, his son and parents. Their pictures were shown all over the news, including a photograph of the little boy.

Obviously, the boy wasn't dead, and while I had a name, what next? All I'd do is get myself killed.

My plan had been to talk to Luca about it when I saw him, have him ask his father questions when he visits next weekend, and maybe we could find a way to make sure the child is safe and free.

"Harper?" Kensley says my name and snaps in front of my face when I don't answer her quickly enough. "What'd you do that upset Luca?"

"I kept something from him," I whisper.

Kensley glances from me to Ashton.

"I'm sure Ashton can talk to Luca. I mean, you said you're roommates with him." Kensley is asking for me, which is sweet, but she has no idea how deep this goes and that talking isn't going to fix the bigger picture.

She's not even privy to the bigger picture, which is that we're to wed, and soon.

I can't lie to Kensley, so not mentioning the wedding seems the best choice.

"Well, I'm sure whatever it was, he'll get over it. If not, there are other guys at EU," Kensley says. "I mean, I'm sure your roommate is a great guy and all, but if he's not the forgiving type, then maybe Ashton can help you meet another great guy. I'm sure he knows a lot of hockey players."

"I'm not dating another athlete," I say and hold up my hand to stop her. "I'm not dating anyone else."

"Okay, then celibacy it is. I can get you a toy rabbit," Kensley says, and I'm not sure if she's joking.

"I'm good, thanks."

"Oh, did you ever get those texts?" Kensley asks me again.

I show her my phone. "Nada." There are no missed texts or even previously read messages from her.

"That's weird," Kensley says. She shows me her phone, and all the text messages came on Saturday morning and they show *read*.

"I didn't have my phone with me when you sent these," I say, noticing the time stamps and the read receipts on them on her phone. They all came when I was out to lunch with Nikki and I had accidentally left my phone behind.

Did Luca read my messages?

Or was it Dante?

The messages aren't anything that would throw up any warnings or even give away that Luca and I hadn't been on a proper date yet.

But the invasion of privacy sits heavily in my stomach.

"It looks like someone read and erased my texts. Do you know anything about this?" I ask, staring at Ashton, imploring him to tell me everything. He was at home with Luca. Surely, he knows something.

"Nope." Ashton shrugs nonchalantly.

Why did I expect him to be helpful?

We finish lunch, and Kensley grabs her backpack and glances at me over her shoulder as we head outside. "You're coming over tonight. We can play some games after dinner." She's not really asking, she wants to hang out, and I neglected her all weekend.

"It's a date."

Ashton is right beside me, and he leans in and whispers, "Don't let Luca hear you say that; he will definitely get jealous."

I glare at Ashton. "Don't you have somewhere else to be?"

"Don't be rude!" Kensley says and purses her lips. "You're welcome to join us if you like. I really want to play D&D if Harper will be dungeon master, and the game isn't any fun with just two people."

Kensley is giving me the look, like she's begging. "We really need three or four to make it fun," I remind her.

"I wouldn't be caught dead playing *that* game," Ashton grumbles. "I have a reputation to uphold, but you girls should come over tonight and we can find something else to play."

I glance up at him, not sure what he's insinuating. I know Ashton's a flirt, and if he's suggesting some kinky sex game with Kensley or me, I'll kick him in the balls.

"We have Catan, Dominion, a bunch of other non-party games. I hate those shitty card games," he mutters.

"Probably because you're bad at them," Kensley quips.

I can't help but laugh, enjoying that she's dishing it out at Ashton.

"I've got to head to class," Kensley says. "But text me the address and we can all hang out this evening, that's fine."

My stomach somersaults at the idea of hanging out over Ashton's place. "Will Luca be there?"

He doesn't want to see me. At least that's all I can assume, based on him not answering my texts and not showing up in class.

He's avoiding me.

Maybe it would be good to see him, to try to talk with him and figure things out. If not for my own sake, then for Zeke's.

Ashton shrugs. "I'm not his babysitter. You guys coming, or what?"

"You don't have practice tonight?"

"We're meeting up in the gym in an hour, but after dinner, we're free. Come over around seven this evening."

"We'll be there," Kensley agrees as she hurries off to class.

I glance at Ashton, rolling my lips together as we walk. I head back to the dorms to study, I'm not sure where he's heading, but he's following me.

"What?" he asks, sensing I have something to say.

"You're really not going to tell me how Luca is doing?"

Ashton exhales heavily and glances around. It's just the two of us on the pavement, no one within listening distance if that's what he's worried about. "I'm not sure what there is to tell. He's pissed as shit."

"At me," I say, not really asking.

"At you, at the universe. I'm not his biggest fan at the moment, either, it turns out. He threw a knife at me on Saturday when he came home."

"Holy shit." My breath catches in my throat as I stop walking and glance him over. "Are you okay?"

Ashton beams. "I'm fine. I know how to duck. He, though, clearly isn't okay. You and he need to figure things out. Have you told your parents yet?"

His question catches me out of the blue, and I walk away, continuing to the dorms.

Ashton takes two quick steps to catch up with me.

"Why are you asking about my parents?" Shivers run down my spine, and while it's chilly outside and the slight breeze tickles my skin, this feeling is beneath my jacket.

"It's common knowledge from the weekend that you're bringing your parents to meet theirs. You do have a wedding to plan," he says and nudges me.

"Fuck off." I quicken my pace, the dorms in the distance.

Why is he still walking with me? His place is in the opposite direction, and there's no reason for him to have parked all the way out here, assuming he has a car. I've never seen him drive.

"I'm trying to help you," Ashton says. He's taller than I am, his long legs easily striding to keep up and match my pace.

It sucks being average height right now. I never cared much, either way, but how easily he walks alongside me while I feel like I have to speed walk to get away. "I don't need your help."

"Fine," Ashton says and stops walking.

Is he finally backing off?

"I'll see you tonight," he shouts at me as I keep hurrying toward the dorms.

"Sure, fine, whatever!" I shout back at him.

He's right, though, at least about the part regarding my parents. I do need to reach out to them, and not just to have a friendly little chat.

But how am I going to break the news of my engagement when they don't even know about Luca?

They're going to be so pissed and so disappointed.

Maybe I wait to tell them about the upcoming wedding and stick to the basics, at least as long as possible. If I can make them realize that Luca is a great guy, assuming he's willing to go along with it, we can have a nice family dinner with both of our families.

Who am I kidding?

A nice family dinner wouldn't involve the mafia.

———

Kensley and I wander up to Luca and Ashton's place for game night. Kensley has a bag slung over her shoulder with a bunch of games.

I'm feeling less than prepared, since I didn't bring anything with me. It's not like I have a stack of board games in my dorm room, which, apparently, Kensley keeps housed under her bed.

I knock on the front door, waiting for Ashton to let us in.

Shivering, I shove my hands back into my pockets to keep warm.

Luca tosses open the front door, glares at us, and then slams it in our faces.

"Jerk!" Kensley shouts.

There's a rumbling of voices on the other end. Clearly, Ashton and Luca are fighting, probably about me.

A few seconds later, Ashton yanks open the door and steps aside. "Sorry about that. My roommate got up on the wrong side of the bed this week."

Luca's glaring at me and then at Ashton. "What's going on?" Luca asks, noticing that it's not just me showing up, but Kensley too.

"Game night!" Kensley says, grinning. She holds up her bag of assorted board games. I swear she's trying to help break the tension. She's a good friend, I'll give her that. And she doesn't even know why things are so tense right now with Luca and me.

"You invited *her* over?" Luca groans, gesturing at me.

Ashton waves us into the living room, and the entire time, Luca is glaring at Ashton, not even hiding his disapproval. "I'm going to kill you," he mutters under his breath.

"Doubtful." Ashton smirks a little too boldly, and Luca lunges at him, grabbing him by the lapels.

"I'm going to fucking end you, Ash," Luca growls.

Ashton doesn't fight back. They're wrestling around, no punches being flung, at least not yet, but Ashton knocks Luca onto the ground and Luca takes him down with him.

"Enough!" I shout at the two of them on the floor.

Luca grumbles and releases his grip on Ashton, getting up and taking a step back. He runs a hand through his hair, and I can see the fog of confusion in his gaze, like he's not sure what just made him attack his friend.

"Kensley, can you and Ashton set up a game?" I ask while I grab Luca's arm, dragging him down the hallway.

"Get off me," Luca grumbles, shaking my arm off him, but he obliges, leading me into his bedroom.

I step in first, him quickly behind, and then he slams the door and the walls shake.

FOUR

LUCA

What the hell are Kensley and Harper doing showing up tonight?

The thoughts that swim through my head fill me with unbridled rage. Has she been hanging around with Ashton?

For how long?

It's clear *he* invited her over with her friend.

"What are you doing hanging around with *him*?" I'm struggling not to scream at Harper, because that's all I want to do.

Shout at her.

Demand her to tell me why she lied to me.

And force her to confess all her secrets, because if she hid Zeke from me, what else is she hiding?

"How long have you and Ashton been hooking up?"

She scoffs and backs up, but her back is against the door. She has nowhere to go, nowhere to run. Even if she tried, we'd find her. The mafia won't let her escape after all she's seen.

She's a liability.

And problems get removed.

"I'm not sleeping with your friend," Harper says.

I step closer, staring into her darkened gaze, trying to decipher if she's lying to me.

But I'm no interrogator.

I couldn't even tell when she had kept the truth about Zeke from me. How the hell am I going to work for the mafia when I can't discern secrets from the truth?

My hand caresses her cheek, holding her jaw to me, glaring at her. "Prove it to me," I seethe.

Her brow furrows as she contemplates how to answer. "I can't. That's impossible."

The heat between us fills the small space, and my heart pounds wildly in my chest.

I will not kiss Harper McKenna.

Her lips are luscious and thick. A soft puff of air spills past, and I lean in, closing half the distance, but I wait, and like a rubber band, I'm being yanked back to reality.

"You lied to me. How am I supposed to believe you now?" I demand. One hand caresses her cheek, the other traps her against the door, keeping her from going anywhere.

"Trust goes both ways, Luca." Her voice is soft, fueled with warmth. She meets my stare, unafraid of me.

She should be afraid.

I'm the son of Dante Ricci.

Her hands are on my waist, her touch is firm yet gentle, her fingers skimming the hem of my shirt.

She creates a fire building within me, yearning for her.

"I know you hate me," Harper says. "I can live with that, but will you condemn my son to death?"

I pull back.

Her son.

Zeke.

I need space to breathe.

Air.

I keep distance between us and fumble back toward my bed, falling to the edge as my knees give out and I struggle to function.

Harper watches me, but she doesn't move closer. "You lied to me too," she says, her voice calm, but I feel the betrayal. "This wouldn't have happened if I'd known the truth about your family."

"You're blaming me." My gaze shoots up at her. "You were the one who snuck into the basement and let that kid out. You nearly got both of us killed!"

I can't admit that she nearly got herself killed and I would have been the one forced to pull the trigger.

I swore I'd never become my father.

If she dies, I die.

But this isn't some Romeo and Juliet bullshit.

Right now, I don't even like her. And I'm pretty sure Romeo loved Juliet.

How's that for tragic?

Me, forced to marry a girl I don't love to protect her. But I don't love her.

I tip my head back, staring up at the ceiling, and sigh. I really wish we had a hockey game tonight. I could use the time on the ice. Lifting weights wasn't enough to stave off the excess energy that she's building within me.

"What are we going to do about next weekend, dinner?" Harper asks.

"Cancel it. You're not stepping foot back into that house," I say. All she'll do is wind up dead.

"I don't think your parents are just going to accept that our engagement is over," Harper says. "They threatened my son, Luca. Maybe you don't care about what happens to him, but I do."

"That's not fair," I growl at her and leap up from the bed. I'm just inches from her face, and I can feel her breath caress my cheek.

My body craves her as I lean closer, but my mind knows better.

If there were any other way out of this mess, I'd jump at it.

Marrying Harper wouldn't be the worst thing in the world if she didn't have a son. But putting Zeke's life in my hands, it's dangerous.

When I'm ordered to kill men, how can I not turn into the man I despise most of all? I don't want that for her son.

"Tell me what I'm supposed to do, Luca." Her voice is soft and filled with concern. Her brow is etched with worry. "I'd leave this place all behind, take Zeke with me, but you said there was nowhere I could go that your family wouldn't find me."

She's right; there is no escape for either one of us that doesn't end with us buried six feet deep.

Reluctantly, I reach for her hands. Her fingers are cold, and I feel the slight tremble as I intertwine our fingers together. "We put on a show, for your parents, for mine."

"You're willing to do that, for me?" Harper asks.

"I told you I'd protect you, that means your son as well."

————

Standing outside of Harper's dorm room, she has her backpack over one shoulder and a duffel bag in her hand.

"No Quinn today?" I ask, noticing her roommate isn't in the room. I'm more than relieved. After Quinn practically tackled me at the front door, shoved her lips on me, and landed me in hot water with Harper, I don't want to run into that succubus.

"Haven't seen her the last two days. She's been by the room; she dropped some things on her bed earlier, but I'm guessing she's found a new boytoy to hook up with. Maybe she's finally sleeping with him at his place!"

Sounds like good news for her. I hope it continues for both of us this evening.

"Are you ready to go?"

"Yeah, I have everything, including an extra change of clothes." She shows me the duffel bag in her hand.

"What? You don't need all that, Harper. It's just dinner tonight."

"You're spending the weekend at your parents'. I figured since you're my ride there, I would be too."

Absolutely not.

"I'll drive you back to campus after dinner."

"That's an extra two hours round trip," Harper says. "If you really don't want me to stay over, I'll just take the bus."

"I don't know how long dinner will be, and there's zero chance, if it's the bus around midnight, that you're getting on that one alone. I'll drive you," I insist.

While the bus system from Breckenridge down to Evergreen is relatively safe, I wouldn't trust Harper to ride it alone past about ten o'clock at night. There are some sketchy guys in our town, and a woman alone? I absolutely won't fathom it.

"Fine." She drops her duffel beside her bed. "I suppose I don't need my books then, either, if I'm not staying with you this weekend." But she pauses before leaving her bag. "On second thought, just in case."

"Just in case, what?" I ask. She's refusing to relinquish her books. Is it because she's struggling in economics again? One week without studying together, and she's already looking a little stressed. Or maybe it's tonight that has her worked up.

"You're not going to need the books, Harper. Leave them here."

She sighs and places the backpack on her bed. "I really need to study this weekend. We have a quiz next week, and I'm going to be so royally screwed."

"What class?" I ask.

She glares at me. "Economics. Do you not pay attention anymore when we're in class? Our professor said we have a quiz coming up, that it'll be on last week's lectures."

I never really started paying attention in that class. The tension between us has gotten a little bit better over the last few days. While I had skipped economics earlier in the week, after our little chat in my bedroom, I relented and showed up in class later in the week.

Honestly, it's not like I even need to show up. I could glance at the book or just remember everything I learned in high school. The concepts are all the same, nothing's changed. I'm certainly not learning anything new.

At least it makes for an easy passing grade.

I haven't spent any time alone with Harper, which means no study sessions as of late. I haven't been in the mood to be overly helpful with her. After all, I'm already keeping her alive. Isn't that enough?

But the look of concern on her face and the fact that she is becoming my problem, I need her to keep her grades up so that she can retain her scholarship.

"I can't study this weekend, unless it's Sunday night after I get back on campus. I'm not even sure what time I'll be home." I don't want to stay the weekend, let alone learn anything about my father's business.

He's a murderer.

What's there to know?

We head to the car and climb in. She buckles in and then glances at me. "How was your game last night?"

"Good." It's the one thing that brings a genuine smile to my face. "Kind of wish it was tonight so that we wouldn't have to make the drive this weekend," I admit.

Most of our hockey games are played on Fridays and Saturdays, which, during the season, saves me some time away from my father. Had we played on Thursday, I'd have been forced to spend Friday night through Sunday under my father's roof.

At least playing Friday cuts one of those days off, and Saturday games make it so I don't have to show up that weekend.

I couldn't be that lucky today.

"I heard you guys won," Harper says.

I glance at her, surprised she knew anything at all. She swears she hates hockey, but I caught her once at one of my games. I keep hoping that she'll show up again.

"We did. Like I said, it was good." I beam.

I scored two goals, which made it pretty damn spectacular after the previous week when I flubbed up.

"No time in the penalty box?" she asks, glancing at me.

A sly smile spreads across my face. "I didn't say that."

Harper laughs, and for the first time in a week, it actually feels like maybe we can get through this tonight.

"When are you coming to see me play?" I glance at her, hoping that she'll show up next week. It'll be another Friday game, which sucks that I'll have to spend Saturday and Sunday back at the compound, but I know what I'm in for.

"Hockey is boring, Luca."

I should be offended. "You don't like watching guys fight on the ice?" My attention is on the road, but I want it to be on her. The fact that she's even asking about hockey has me filled with curiosity and tingles of warmth.

Is this her way of trying to make peace after all that's happened?

"I don't like worrying that you're going to get hurt," she says.

My gaze meets hers briefly before I return my focus to the road. "You don't have to worry about me, Harper. I can take care of myself on the ice. I've been playing for years."

"I know," she says and glances out the window. "I just don't want to see you get hurt."

"Before we met, did you ever like to watch guys fight on the ice? A lot of girls find it a real turn-on." The number of puck bunnies who follow us from game to game is intense.

"Sorry, I'm not one of those girls who drools over guys fighting. I don't like boxing or MMA, either."

Fair enough. I'm glad she's not a glutton for other people's pain.

Silence fills the car, and she shifts again, her hands tapping nervously on her lap. "You should know, Luca, that I didn't mention the engagement to my parents."

Well, that's going to make things hell awkward when my parents inevitably bring it up. "Why not?"

Harper shifts in the seat and sighs. "There is zero chance that they'd have gotten on board with coming tonight if I told them I'm engaged."

"Even if you mentioned that he's the most amazing guy you've ever met."

She laughs and grins. "He's modest too."

"Seriously, Harper, what did you tell your parents about us?" We're only a few minutes out from the compound and *now* we're having this conversation.

My grip tightens on the steering wheel, and my shoulder muscles tighten. I can feel my muscles in my neck arguing with me to lighten my hold on the steering wheel, but it seems impossible.

"I mentioned that we met on campus, that you've been helping me in economics, tutoring me. They know you're a year older, and I mentioned that we had dinner with your parents last weekend, and they want to get to know my parents."

"Okay, all truths," I say, realizing it will definitely be

easier if we don't have to create too many fabrications to keep track of.

"Anything else?" I ask. While she may not have mentioned the engagement, I'm curious how serious her parents think our relationship is at the moment.

"I told them that I really like you and to be nice."

"All good things to mention." I exhale nervously and glance at Harper. "Is Zeke coming tonight?"

"Yes, my son will be joining us for dinner. I tried gently suggesting that maybe we could find him a sitter for the evening, but they insisted that Zeke come, since he's family, and my son."

"It'll be fine," I say and reach for Harper's hand, trying to reassure her that her son will be safe.

"Will it?" She stares at me. I can feel the worry on her shoulders. "Honestly, Luca, I really was hoping we could push the parents meeting back and have you meet them and Zeke first."

That would have been the safer option and might have even helped for tonight's dinner, but my parents had insisted that we all dine together. "Dante would never go for that. He wants to watch the madness unfold in front of him."

"Seriously?" Harper asks. "I just assumed he was afraid I'd spill the secret about the mafia or the little boy being held in the basement—"

She is right. I'm sure that had been on the forefront of my father's mind, concerned that he couldn't control her if she's not under his roof. It's why he had originally demanded we stay until we were wed.

That was until he realized Harper was good at keeping secrets. She'd kept Zeke from me. From everyone at Evergreen University.

"You can't mention the little boy in the basement."

"I know, but—"

"No." I shut that down immediately. "You can't mention the kid. I'll—look into it while I'm working for Dante," I say.

"You will?" Her voice catches with a ray of hope.

"Just let me deal with the mafia stuff. You stay out of trouble, please." I don't want to have to worry about Harper all evening. It's going to be enough to try to get through dinner with both of our parents.

"I promise not to step foot in that prison basement again."

I snort. "Good."

I hate the cost of what it took for her to learn her lesson.

A price we are all forced to pay.

FIVE

LUCA

It's cloudy outside, and as we arrive at the compound, large drops of rain begin cascading down from the heavens.

It fits my mood perfectly.

There's a vehicle in front of the house that I don't recognize. It's a small, two-door black sedan with quite some age on it. The dark sheen has seen better days, as has the front corner bumper.

"Your parents' car?" I ask, my stomach tumbling at the fact that they arrived before us.

I grab an umbrella from the backseat and walk around to lead Harper out of the car, sheltering her from the rain.

She raises an eyebrow as I wrap my arm around her waist. I lean down, my lips brush against her ear. "Fake dating, remember," I say. "We need to make this convincing tonight."

"Yes," she whispers.

While my parents probably don't care whether we're an actual couple or not, we are clearly performing for her parents this evening.

I lead her up to the main door, and before I can so much as knock, the front door swings open and one of my father's men greets us. There's not so much as a smile on his face.

"Come inside," Vito says. "Everyone is in the family room."

I lead Harper into the house, and we both take off our shoes and coats. I reach for her hand as I lead her down the hallway to the open room on the left beside the dining room.

"Mama!" Zeke squeals and throws up his arms at Harper the second he lays eyes on her.

She untangles her hand from mine and hurries over to her son, bringing him into her arms, nuzzling and kissing him as she puts him on her hip to hold.

"We were just talking about the two of you," Dante says.

It's not much of a greeting. Not that I'd expect much from my father.

My mother, Nikki, gets up from her seat on the sofa and embraces me in a tight squeeze before untangling her grip and giving Harper a much gentler hug with Zeke in-hand.

Harper's parents are both nursing a beer, and I have a feeling we're going to need something far stronger to deal with tonight. Her mother is standing near Harper, keeping a close eye on Zeke while her father sits beside my old man on the sofa up against the wall.

"Hi, I'm Luca," I say, introducing myself to her mother first, as she's a few feet closer to me. I hold out my hand to properly introduce myself. Her gaze tightens, but she forces a smile.

She has Harper's eyes, the same dark, mysterious gaze crosses her features, and I can't tell if she already hates me. I get the distinct impression that she's made up her mind about me, perhaps before even meeting.

I glance at Dante, hoping he didn't mention the engagement.

Perhaps we can skirt through dinner with zero mention of it.

"I'm Catrina," Harper's mother says and gestures toward her husband, "and that is Jack. He's enthralled in a heated business discussion on stocks, bonds, and gold as an asset. They'd be putting me to sleep if it weren't for this little one—" She runs a hand through Zeke's dainty brown hair.

He reaches an arm out for Catrina before Harper manages to recapture his attention.

It's hard not to stare at the bond between Harper and Zeke.

She's completely immersed in his little world, cooing and talking to him, as she covers him with kisses. "Do you want to meet someone special to me?" she whispers in the sweetest and most precious voice.

Zeke doesn't seem to care much either way. He's squirming and probably wants to run around like a maniac. I'm sure my parents would love that. Another McKenna to discover something they shouldn't in this place.

Except he wouldn't be able to spill any secrets, given that he doesn't seem to be talking much. It's a lot more like babbling.

Every so often, I can make out a word he's trying to say, like *mama,* but mostly it's nonsense to my ears.

Harper steps closer, bringing Zeke right over to me. "Luca, this is my son, Zeke. Zeke, can you say hi to Luca?" She takes Zeke's hand, which is wrapped around her thumb, and bounces it up and down in a wave-like gesture.

Zeke looks at me curiously, his wide eyes enraptured with me.

"Hi, buddy," I say, unsure what to do.

Zeke immediately buries his face in her neck.

Did I say something wrong?

"You don't have to be shy," Harper says and rubs her son's back. "Luca is a very special friend."

Zeke glances up briefly from Harper's chest before meeting my stare and then hiding again.

The kid already hates me.

Great.

I force a smile and then stalk across the room to properly introduce myself to Harper's father. "Hi, I'm Luca," I say, holding out my hand.

"I'm Jack," her father says, his gaze tight. There's no smile, no hint of happiness. He already doesn't like me and we just met. "How about you and I take a walk outside?"

"Okay," I say with a nod, but my insides are warning me not to do it.

Jack puts his beer down on a coaster on the end table and stands, stretching.

I glance at Harper, and her brow pinches, clearly worried as well. "Hey," she says, bouncing Zeke in her arms as she approaches Jack and me.

I press a chaste kiss at the corner of her lips, trying to make our fake relationship believable. Actually, kissing her would be better, but she does have a toddler in her arms, and that's the excuse I'm going with for not making out with her, because in reality, I'm still pissed and hurting about her betrayal.

She lied to me about Zeke.

But I have to bury that anger for tonight.

"We're just going to take a walk," I say, gesturing at her father.

Harper frowns and turns her attention toward her father. "Dad, it's raining outside. You're not taking Luca into the rain for a talk. You can sit down in here and get to know one another."

I'm surprised that she's so brazen with her father, but of course, he isn't mafia. She doesn't have to fear him.

"Of course," Jack says and forces a smile, but his eyes don't shine. "I didn't realize it started to rain."

I head for the couch and grab a seat next to Jack.

Dante scoots over, leaving me some space.

It'd be great if he got up, went to talk to Mom or even Catrina. But instead, he's hanging out with us, probably eavesdropping, not that it takes much with him sitting beside us.

"My daughter called us this week to tell us about her new boyfriend," Jack says. He reaches for his beer, the bottle nestled between his hands as he glances at it. "Can't say I'm happy with all of her life choices."

"You mean Zeke?"

Jack turns toward me. "I mean my fifteen-year-old daughter getting knocked up by her eighteen-year-old loser boyfriend in high school. Best thing he did for Harper was turn over his parental rights."

"You don't have to worry. Harper and I are adults; we know about safe sex."

My father clears his throat behind me, like he's trying not to choke. Maybe he should quit listening in and get up, go bother someone else.

But Dante doesn't move from his position on the couch.

Jack holds up a hand to stop me from discussing anything further. "I don't need to hear about you fucking my little girl. I need you to understand that she's a mom, first and foremost. Zeke comes before any boyfriend, so if you think you're in it for a good time, you're going to be sorely disappointed."

"I can assure you, Mr. McKenna, that I care deeply about your daughter. I'm grateful for the opportunity to get to meet you, your wife, and Zeke this evening." I'm doing everything I can to remain calm and not screw this up with her parents.

I can't see them giving us their blessing. Already he doesn't particularly like me, and I haven't even mentioned our engagement.

"It'll take time for us to see what kind of man you really are," Jack says. He glances past me at Dante.

"I mean no disrespect to you, Dante. I'm sure you raised a wonderful son," Jack says, trying to be polite, "but understand that I have to look out for my daughter and my grandson."

I don't dare turn around to witness the expression on my father's face. "I understand quite a lot about protecting family," Dante says. The sofa dips, and I realize that he's standing up. "Perhaps we should all take this conversation to the dining room; dinner will be served soon."

I stand and hurry over to Harper; my hand falls to her lower back. She's still holding Zeke in her arms, but he seems to be busy playing with a toy phone in his hands.

"We're moving this party into the dining room," I say. I would offer to help hold Zeke, but I doubt he'd let me, since I'm a stranger to the kid.

"Oh good. I could really use a sit," Harper admits and then groans. "Not again."

"What's wrong?" I ask, noticing her frustration when she lifts Zeke and wetness is dripping down his legs and onto her clothes.

"I'll find you something of mine to wear. Why don't you get him cleaned up in the bathroom?" I offer.

"Can you grab the diaper bag? It's over by the door," Harper asks.

I grab the bag and lead her out of the family room and to the bathroom. I don't want her wandering around and finding trouble. Although the fact that her parents were invited today means that it's probably pretty calm around here.

"I'll grab my bag from the car," I say and hurry down the hallway after she's situated. I slip on my shoes and run out into the rain, getting soaked while I retrieve my duffel.

I probably should have grabbed the umbrella, but I was trying to be quick. I ditch my shoes inside and leave a wet trail behind me as I slosh across the hall. Even my socks are soaked. I knock on the bathroom door. "It's just me," I say.

"It's unlocked," Harper answers.

I turn the handle and step in, bringing the bag with me.

Her back is to me, and she's got Zeke on the bathroom mat with a changing pad, as she secures the tabs on his new diaper. "All clean," she says in that sweet voice that she uses when talking to Zeke.

He's squirming and restless, but she manages to keep him steady while she changes his clothes, since the other ones were wet.

Something we both have in common, well kind of.

Mine is definitely from the rain, though, kid.

Harper lifts him off the changing mat and turns him to face me. I scrunch my nose, making a face at the little fellow, and he laughs and claps his hands together.

Cute.

"Can you hold him while I change?" Harper asks. She puts her arms out with him in her grasp, handing him off like a football.

"I—um, if you need me to," I stumble with what to say. It's not that I mind holding Zeke, that's the furthest thought from my mind. I just don't want him to cry or be scared of me.

I take the toddler from her arms, and immediately, the tears start, as does the screaming.

Exactly what I was afraid of.

"It's okay, buddy. Your mom is right here," I say and turn him around to face her. That seems to settle him for the moment, at least from the tears.

He squirms in my grasp, wanting to be in her arms. "Mama. Mama," he chants repeatedly, trying to get her attention.

"I know, Zeke. Just a minute."

Harper unzips my duffel and rummages through the clothes. "What are you going to wear?" she asks, her gaze moving over my soaking wet ensemble.

"It's fine. I'm only covered in rainwater."

She yanks out my t-shirt and cargo pants for tomorrow. I doubt the cargo pants will fit her. "Turn around," she demands, gesturing with her finger for me to spin around.

I turn Zeke and myself around, and the crying ensues.

"Aww, come on, Zeke. I'm not that bad to look at," I say and spin him around to face me. I attempt to make silly faces at him, scrunching my nose and then sticking out my tongue. Nothing helps.

The soft thud of clothes hits the floor.

"He clearly wants you," I say, turning back around because I can't stand the sound of Zeke crying and screaming for Harper. It breaks my heart.

Harper's eyes widen when she sees me staring at her in her bra and panties.

"Oh my gosh, Luca! Shut your eyes," she snaps at me.

"It's not like I haven't seen it before," I say with a smirk.

I close my eyes but keep Zeke in my arms, turning him around to see Harper, which at least makes the crying stop.

"Yeah, well, you don't get a free show," Harper grumbles at me.

A few seconds later, her hand grazes mine. "You can open them now," she says.

I hand over Zeke, who gladly climbs into his mother's arms. I don't know how she manages to spend so much time away from him. It probably can't be easy for her.

"I'll get your clothes washed during dinner," I say and gather her belongings. I lead her to the dining room, drop her off with the others, while I hurry across the hall to the laundry room.

I quickly toss her clothes in the washer before returning to keep her company.

There's no sign of Moreno, Nikki, or Nova for dinner this evening. If I had to guess, Dante suggested they go out to eat. It's not as though Moreno is doing much work this evening with Harper's parents under their roof.

"You have a lovely house," Catrina says as she takes a seat across from us at the dining room table. Her husband sits beside her, with Dante next to him, and Nikki sits across from him.

I grab the seat next to Mom, hoping to make it a little easier for Harper if I'm between Mom and her.

Harper sits with Zeke on her lap.

"Can I make anything special for Zeke?" Nikki asks after everyone's seated.

"There's plenty of food," Harper says, noticing the spread on the table of everything from mashed potatoes and squash to roasted chicken and brisket. "He'll be fine."

Everyone serves themselves, passing the dishes around. I help dish out food on Harper's plate since she's holding Zeke and he keeps reaching for everything on the table.

I don't know what she likes to eat. I also don't have any idea if Zeke has any allergies. She hasn't mentioned anything, so I'm hoping everything on the table is okay to serve her.

I fill her plate with enough food to feed two adults.

"That's more than enough, Luca." She laughs as I keep heaping more potatoes onto her plate. Those have to be a safe food for Zeke. I don't want him choking on dinner. "Are you trying to feed a hockey team?"

"Well, in case he likes it, I wanted you to have enough."

"Did I just hear hockey?" Jacks asks, grabbing my attention. "Do you play?"

"Yeah, I play for the Narwhals," I say, putting enough food on my own plate for myself now that I've taken care of Harper. "I'd love to go pro someday."

"Isn't that every hockey player's dream?" Dante says without the slightest hint of admiration for me.

Can't say I'm surprised.

He's made it known that he despises the sport and, even more so, my career aspirations. But it's not like all of that matters anymore.

"Please, feel free to start," Nikki says as she gestures toward everyone's plates. She's still dishing out her own meal onto her plate, but she's trying to make sure that the guests know they can start eating.

Catrina smiles, her gaze on Zeke. "What are your plans after college if you don't make it onto a professional team?"

"The realist," Nikki says with a soft laugh.

Dante's cold stare is on me, waiting to hear what I say. "I plan on joining the family business."

"Oh," Jack says. "What is it you guys do?" He turns his attention to Dante, waiting for him to explain his profession and endeavors.

I take the opportunity to shove food in my mouth, so I'm not forced to talk. If I'm eating, then hopefully they'll leave me well enough alone. Plus, I'm starving. I skipped lunch, big mistake, so I'm more than hungry for dinner.

"We handle quite a bit of temporary contracts and provide support services for those businesses that need assistance," Dante says.

That's my father's code speak for shaking down businesses and offering muscle for those businesses he acquires.

"Sounds quite busy," Jack says, clearly not having any inkling of what Dante does for a living. He glances around the dining room. "But clearly, your business does well. You have a beautiful home."

"Thank you," Mom says. "What about the two of you?" She always knows how to steer the conversation away from trouble.

It's probably wise that Moreno and his family were out for the day. It might seem odd having two families that live and work together under the same roof.

No sense in rousing suspicion with Catrina and Jack.

"I'm home with Zeke," Catrina says, "but I worked as a barista at the ski resort in town since they first opened. I've been with them since new management."

"How do you like the owner?" Dante asks.

"He pays better and takes our suggestions seriously, so I'm happy with the new changes. When Harper graduates and I don't have Zeke full-time, I'll probably go back to work."

"And what do you do, Jack?" Nikki asks, keeping the conversation rolling.

I'm grateful that there hasn't been an inquisition on Harper's and my new relationship. Yet I know there's still time, the night is young.

"I'm a manager for Blue Sky Resort. I handle the hotel side of things, making sure the guests are taken care of," Jack says.

"That sounds wonderful," Nikki says and reaches her hand across the table for Dante. "We've always wanted to spend a weekend at the resort, haven't we, honey?"

Dante grumbles about skiing under his breath but forces a smile to appease my mother.

"You'd like it. We offer both ski and snowboarding lessons for beginners," Jack suggests to Dante. "The spa is great, always makes the wife happy, and they have a pretty decent golf package with the course down the road, if you play and decide you want to come off-season, which is our summer."

"I don't play," Dante says, his tone clipped.

Jack nods and takes a bite of his food.

I lean toward Harper, my breath against her ear as I try to keep our conversation solely between us. "How do you think it's going?" I whisper.

Harper has a small spoonful of mashed potatoes that she's feeding to Zeke.

He keeps reaching for the spoon to feed himself, but she clearly isn't letting him. "Do you want me to feed him while you eat?"

"Would you?" Her eyes widen, and she turns him to face me but keeps him on her lap. "He's super messy, and your parents have carpet in their dining room. I don't want them to kill me when they see the mess he'll make in this place."

If Dad wasn't mafia, I'd say she's overreacting, but I sense her hesitation and fear. I take the spoon, giving him a few more bites of mashed potatoes as she cuts up the roasted chicken into teeny tiny bites.

"You can give him some chicken; otherwise, this little monster will fill up on potatoes." Harper kisses the top of Zeke's head and then stuffs a few bites of dinner into her own mouth.

Her eyes momentarily close, and I can see how hungry she is as she enjoys dinner.

That's the one advantage to having wealthy mafia parents: they have a professional chef who knows how to cook just about anything, and it always tastes divine.

I keep feeding Zeke, moving away from the mashed potatoes and offering him chicken, which he insists on removing from my fork and putting in his hands to feed himself.

I grab my cloth napkin and set it on his lap and cover Harper to keep the mess from spilling everywhere.

"How about I feed you?" I say to Zeke and try another bite of chicken. "Open up, little tiger," I say as I bring the fork to his lips.

Zeke's mouth opens and then his hands clench closed. "Roar!" Zeke mimics a tiger, although it sounds like it could be a bit more of a lion.

But I'm not correcting him, and it gives me the

opportunity to feed him another bite without making a huge mess.

"Don't you miss when Luca was that age?" Mom asks, smiling across the table at Dante.

"I was never this little," I counter, knowing it isn't true but still not believing it when I stare at the little tiger in Harper's arms. He's adorable. I doubt my father was doting on me when I was Zeke's age.

"You certainly weren't that little for long," Mom says. "You had a growth spurt that I swear started when you were eighteen months. You just kept growing."

"Enough about me, please?" I'm practically begging Mom to shut up. I don't need her embarrassing me in front of Harper. Next, she'll be pulling out baby pictures and comparing them to Zeke.

"Fine, fine. You're right, dear. We should be talking about the real reason we're all here this evening, the upcoming nuptials," Mom says.

Jack's fork drops from his hand, hits the porcelain plate and then clammers to the floor. "Excuse me?" His voice is like thunder, completely caught off guard by my mother's comment.

Can't say I'm surprised, since Harper didn't mention it to her parents.

Catrina's eyes are wide, and she reaches for her water glass, bringing it to her lips for a second, startled as well by the mention of nuptials.

Dante remains calm as he doesn't so much as face Catrina and Jack. His stare is entirely on Harper. "My son and your daughter have decided to wed." There's no emotion in his voice, and for once, I can't get a read on him.

This marriage was his idea.

Well, technically, it was mine, in order to save Harper after what she witnessed and had done, but he went along with it.

It never would have gone this far if he hadn't ordered me to execute her.

"Harper?" Catrina puts her fork down. Her hands remain in her lap while the news dawns on her. "Do you care to explain yourself?"

Harper smiles, and while I know she's entirely faking the ever-present happiness, I can't help but fall for it too.

"We're both incredibly happy dating, and we want to see where this next stage of life takes us, together," Harper says.

Okay, not the best line to convince her parents of our engagement.

Jack turns to face Dante. "Did you know about this?"

"They announced their engagement last weekend," Dante says. "It's why we insisted that you join us for dinner this evening."

"You're engaged?" Catrina balks, clearly hurt. "We didn't even know you were dating anyone! You talk to us every week, you talk on video chat with Zeke, you never thought once to tell us about Luca?"

"It all happened quite so suddenly this semester," Harper says. "I care about Luca immensely."

"And if he cares about you," Catrina says, "then he'll wait to marry you. There is no reason for the two of you to rush into such a life-long decision."

Harper glances at me, her breathing slightly erratic. I can hear the first telltale signs of her panicking and want to embrace her, hold her tight against me, and let her know that we'll figure this out together.

But Zeke is still situated on her lap, and somehow, I'm mindlessly feeding him bite after bite of chicken. He doesn't seem to notice or at least understand what is happening at the table.

To him, it's just more yummy food time.

"We could certainly wait," I say and feel the wrath of my father's stare. "But when you love someone and you know that they're the only one you want to spend the rest of your life with, why wait?"

"Because there's a child involved!" Catrina says. "Are you telling me that you're honestly ready to be a father?"

I stare at Zeke, and while I know nothing about two-year-olds or what it means to raise a child, I know that one day I do want to become a father. I just vow never to become *my* father.

"I'm not asking him to be a father," Harper says before I have time to answer.

"Well, you ought to be," Catrina says. "Because if you're marrying Luca, then Zeke is moving in with you. I don't need to be taking care of your son if you think you're ready for marriage."

"Mom," Harper whispers, realizing what that means about her pursuing her education.

"We've thought about that as well," Mom says, glancing at Dante. "We've procured a place on campus that meets the requirements of Harper's scholarship and isn't part of the dorms. Harper and Luca will be able to have Zeke living with them beginning in January."

Jack frowns, shaking his head. "So, you're in agreement with the two of them getting hitched? My daughter is eighteen. She has her entire life ahead of her."

"Your daughter is a mother," Dante says curtly. "I'm giving her the opportunity to raise her son *and* go to college. It'll build character."

"Don't tell me how to raise my daughter," Catrina scoffs and stands. "It's time to go," she says to Jack.

"Gladly." Jack scoots his chair back and gets to his feet.

"Mom," Harper's voice trails off, "can we please sit back down and talk?"

"Absolutely not." Catrina strides to the other side of the table. I think she's going to take Zeke from Harper, but I'm not sure exactly what will happen.

This whole dinner went exactly how I'd expect an epic disaster to go.

"If you think you're ready to be a wife, then you're clearly ready to be a mother." Catrina leans down and kisses Zeke's cheek. "I'll retrieve the car seat so that you can take him home with you."

"I'm taking him back to the dorms?" Harper's voice catches in throat. "Mom, I can't do that."

"Perhaps your boyfriend's parents can help. If you're getting married, then you don't need our support," Catrina says.

"But that's exactly what I need," Harper whispers. "It's why we told you and didn't get married behind your back."

Jack scowls at me. "And we're ever so grateful for your honesty. But we raised you better, Harper. At least we thought we did. First, you get pregnant in high school. We tried to be understanding. We thought sending you to college would help both you and Zeke. And now this? It's like a slap in the face to us. If you want to be married, then it's time you step up and be your son's mother. We're done raising him."

Jack escorts his wife down the hallway, back toward the front door.

Harper is hurrying after them, Zeke in her arms. I'm right on her heel, whether they want me to follow or not.

"Mom, please, at least give us some time," Harper is begging her mom for help and I'm just standing there, unsure how to make any of this right.

It's not like we want to get married, but the fake relationship seems to have just backfired in our faces.

And honesty won't save us.

I can't tell her parents we're doing this because I'm protecting their daughter.

"I love Harper," I say, trying to find the right words to fix this as best I can. "I realize you don't know me yet. I'm sure this all seems sudden, but I want to be a father to Zeke, a husband to Harper, and I vow to protect them until the day I die."

Jack pauses at the front door. I think for a moment I might be getting through to him, and then I realize he's getting his shoes on, and then he helps Catrina with her shoes and coat.

"You kids are jumping headfirst into a lifelong commitment. If you invited us to dinner for our blessing or our approval, you're not getting it," Jack says.

Catrina buttons her coat, and the frown at the corner of her lips is pale compared to her watery eyes. She leans down, kissing Zeke's cheek. "Be good for your mama," Catrina says to her grandson.

"Hate me all you want, but don't do this to your daughter. Don't freeze her out of your life," I say.

"You don't have to worry about us pretending, Luca. We don't like you," Jack says, making his opinion quite clear. "We would never disown our daughter, but we won't be attending the wedding. If you both decide to go through with marrying one another, you're on your own."

"Mom, please. I'll take Zeke as soon as I'm in the new place in January. But I can't just bring him into the dorms, can you help?" Harper is practically begging, and I rest a hand on her back.

"It's okay. We'll figure something out," I say.

Catrina stalls by the door and holds out her arms to Zeke. "Until you move in together. Unless you both come to your senses."

Harper grabs Zeke's shoes and coat, bundling him up before walking him outside to their car and putting him into the back, in his car seat.

I hold the umbrella over Harper, keeping her dry while I watch her say goodbye to Zeke, but at least I know the goodbye isn't forever.

We head back into the house, Harper looking dejected, and I wrap my arms around her, embracing her in a hug.

She buries her face in my neck, and I can feel the soft sobs wrack her body. Soothingly, I rub her back, trying to comfort her as I feel my father's stern gaze on me.

"Luca, a word," Dante says.

"I'll be right back. Stay here," I warn her as I

untangle from her embrace and leave her in the foyer.

She doesn't move as I approach Dante. He keeps me out of earshot, but we're still in sight of Harper. Can't say I'm surprised that he doesn't trust her.

Trust has to be earned.

Those are his words that ruminate through my head, a phrase he repeatedly told me throughout my youth.

"It's late. You should take Harper back to campus, and I'll see you next weekend. When is your next game?" Dante asks.

"Thursday night." I wish it were Friday or Saturday, so that I wouldn't have to spend another minute under *his* roof.

Dante's eyes tighten, and he nods. "Good. Then you'll come on Friday after your classes are finished."

"I have practice Sunday," I remind him.

"You'll leave before the hockey team even notices that you were away."

Somehow, I doubt that. Ashton will know, and surely Liam will notice. And that's assuming Ashton doesn't throw a party at our place, which he's known to do.

"Say goodbye to your mother before you leave," Dante reminds me.

"Let me grab Harper's clothes from the laundry," I say. "Then we'll be on our way."

Within fifteen minutes, we're back in the car, heading back to campus.

"Thanks for the ride," Harper says, glancing at me. She reaches for my hand on the steering wheel, and I oblige.

She's been quiet since we left.

Too quiet if you ask me.

"You really didn't have to drive me all the way back home and then have to go back—"

"I'm not going back," I say, glancing at her for a brief moment. "And you still need to study. Any chance you brought the notes for class?"

"You told me not to bring it with me," Harper says

and untangles her hand from mine. She shifts in her seat.

"I can't tell if you're mad at me," I say.

Her leg bounces restlessly. The girl can't seem to sit still in the front seat. "I'm mad at myself, and I don't want you getting into trouble with your dad. You can't just avoid going back there because he has men—"

I rest my hand on her knee, trying to calm her. "Dante spoke with me before we left. He told me not to worry about staying this weekend, but I'll be there starting Friday through Sunday."

"Oh." She exhales a soft breath.

"Is that relief or more concern?" I ask.

"Can't it be both? I'm glad you don't have to go back there tonight, but I really don't like the idea of you going there at all..."

"I know," I say. It's not like this is the future I envisioned for myself, either, but I'm doing it for *her* and, now, for Zeke as well.

Silence fills the space between us, and I squeeze her thigh before returning my hand to the steering wheel. "Any chance you remember any concepts from our economics quiz?"

"Supply and demand curves," Harper says.

"Oh, that's an easy one."

Harper laughs. "I know, that's why I remember it. That's the only concept I grasped, and it's because you and I went over it a couple of weeks ago. The rest—" she gestures from her head to the window, "flew right out the moment it was explained."

"Okay, when we get back to campus, you'll come over and study with me for an hour or two before I drop you off for the night."

Harper is silent.

"Does that sound okay to you?" I ask.

Her silence has me concerned.

"I was thinking maybe I could stay the night with you. Just for tonight," Harper says. I feel her gaze on me, watching me closely.

My body craves her company, her warmth, the feel of her skin on mine. I've been having dreams about her but *just for tonight* is nowhere near enough.

And then there's Zeke.

Aside from the obvious, that she lied to me about him and kept him a secret, I can't let her get too close to me, to us becoming *real*. Not if I'm forced to work for my father.

Zeke deserves better.

So does Harper.

"I don't think that's a good idea," I say, and my heart hurts when I answer her.

She sighs ever so softly. "You're never going to forgive me, are you?" Her question is hardly above a whisper.

Harper will never understand where I'm coming from, the things I've seen as a child of the mafia, and I don't want that for Zeke.

Anything I can do to protect the family, *my* family—Harper and Zeke—I will. Even if that means breaking hearts.

SIX

HARPER

"When is your next hockey game?" I ask Ashton.

"Why? Looking forward to showing up and cheering me on?"

I toss a fry at him. I'm seated across from Kensley, and Ashton is between us at the lunch table.

It seems like every time I go to grab lunch with Kensley, Ashton keeps showing up uninvited.

"That wasn't my first thought," I quip and laugh.

"Harper's going to be cheering for Luca. Am I right?" Kensley asks, her eyes wiggling suggestively.

She still doesn't know about the upcoming wedding, Zeke, or the new living arrangements in the works.

I've been keeping so much from Kensley, she's going to absolutely hate me when she finds out I've been lying to her.

"Those two are something else," Ashton says between bites of his hamburger. "I swear, the two of you are trying to make my life more difficult."

"Why's that?" Kensley asks. "Did Luca send you here for intel? Because if he's avoiding Harper again—"

I love how protective Kensley is of me. "Luca and I are fine," I say. I grab another fry from my plate and chomp on it. The food is an easy distraction from having to talk about Luca.

"Fine," Kensley repeats. "Usually, fine is like shit is bad, but I don't want to talk about it."

Exactly.

Kensley doesn't seem to give up, though. "We can go to the game, and then are you free this weekend? You ditched me last Saturday. I was hoping we could do a movie marathon of Christmas romances. 'Tis the season."

Inwardly, I grumble, but I force a smile. "I'm free Saturday." I don't elaborate on last weekend.

Ashton is watching me with too much intensity, probably wondering if I'll break.

"What?" I ask, glaring at him.

"Gosh, Harper. You and Luca really aren't shacking up, are you?" Kensley asks.

"Shacking up?" I raise an eyebrow at her choice of words.

Ashton smirks, enjoying the exchange between the two of us. He's eating his burger but fully engrossed in our conversation. I wish he weren't at the table, but short of telling him to move his ass, he doesn't seem like he has any intention of going away anytime soon.

"Don't you start up." I point at him, warning him to keep his trap shut.

Apparently, my threat is enough to elicit a response from him.

"Kensley is right. You just seem really agitated. I think a good fuck would take care of that."

"And you're offering?" I glare at Ashton.

He puts his burger down and holds his hands up in surrender. "I'm not foolish enough to make that proposition. Your boyfriend would kill me."

Kensley glares from Ashton to me. "So, Luca *is* your boyfriend. I knew you two had something going on, but you guys weren't talking, last you told me."

"We're fine," I grumble, really wanting this interrogation between my best friend and Luca's best friend to disappear.

I glare at Ashton. "Is that why you're joining us for lunch all the time?"

He shakes his head, not understanding my question.

"You're Luca's best friend." I state the obvious. "Are you reporting back to him on anything I say?"

"I promise, I'm not reporting anything to Luca," Ashton says. "He's been a bit of an ass around the house. We've been steering clear of one another."

"And on the ice?" I ask.

"At practice, he's in full game mode. Nothing else

seems to matter." Ashton finishes the last bite of his burger. "How'd things go with Zeke this weekend?"

My shoulders tense as I glance from Ashton to Kensley.

Did he really have to namedrop my son?

Is he trying to fuck with me or just make sure that I lose my only friend on campus?

Kensley glances from Ashton to me. "Who's Zeke? Is that why you ditched me this weekend? For another guy?" Her cheeks redden, and I can feel that she's growing angry with me. "And didn't you just say you're dating Luca? What the hell, Harper?"

I push my tray of fries away. I'm no longer hungry.

Ashton smirks and steals one off my plate.

How juvenile of him.

"So, who is Zeke?" Kensley asks again, and I can sense her frustration.

"He's my son," I say, avoiding her glare.

Kensley pauses for a moment, tilts her head, and stares at me, perplexed. "You have a son," she repeats the phrase slowly, as it sinks in. "Where is he now?" Her tone is soft, her voice a strange comfort in that she's not freaking out at me.

At least not yet.

"He lives with my parents until next semester."

It's like a Band-Aid that has to be yanked off, revealing everything to her.

"What's next semester?" Kensley asks.

"The wedding," Ashton says, leaning back in his chair and smirking.

"Bastard," I mutter at him. I reach for my fries and throw a fistful at him.

Ashton doesn't even attempt to dodge them. He just lets them fall against his chest. He brushes them off, not the least bit insulted by what I've done.

"Wait. You're getting married? Is it to Luca? Is Luca the father?" Kensley asks, trying to wrap her head around the announcement.

"Luca isn't the father, but, yes, we're engaged," I say quite calmly.

"Give me your hand," she says and yanks my arm across the table, disappointment etched on her face. "No ring?"

How is Kensley so calm about the news of the engagement? I had expected her to scream at me, to tell me that I was making the biggest mistake of my life.

"It's not like we're rolling around in cash," I joke and withdraw my hand from hers, placing it back into my lap. "His mom offered to buy us wedding bands, as a gift."

"That's nice," Kensley says slowly, like her brain is wrapping around the entire scenario. "What about your parents? And your son? And I have so many freaking questions, Harper."

Ashton doesn't say a word; he just watches and listens. I'm not sure what Luca told him, if anything, about last weekend when we went to visit his parents and had dinner with both of our families.

"My parents aren't exactly on board, and since the news of the engagement, they're pushing Zeke back on me."

"Well, he is your son," Kensley says. "Wait. How old is he?"

"Two," I say and sigh, retrieving my phone from my pocket. I flip through my pictures and reveal a photo of Zeke with a huge, toothy grin. In the picture, he's trying to reach for my phone, and rather close-up, with his face near the camera lens.

"Gosh, he's adorable. Makes my uterus hurt," Kensley says with a laugh.

Ashton snorts and then holds out his hand, wanting to see the photo that I showed Kensley. "He's actually cute," Ashton says, sounding quite surprised.

"Thanks?" I laugh and put my phone back into my pocket. "He's a handful. Mom stayed home after I gave birth, while I finished up high school and got my diploma. She agreed to help me raise him while I went to college. Long story, but I try to visit him on weekends when I don't have to study. When I don't see him, I have video calls with him, so he remembers who I am."

"I'm sure he knows who you are," Kensley says and smiles weakly. "I really wish you'd have trusted me to tell me sooner about your son, but I'm sure that was a huge secret to carry."

The truth is, I didn't want Zeke to be a secret, but it had been my parents' idea. They'd wanted me to keep it quiet in high school. I'd been homeschooled the minute my parents discovered I was pregnant and then, after Zeke was born, the following year, I returned to high school.

I suppose they were trying to give me a normal life.

At least that's what I'd thought, but I think it had more to do with my education, them wanting to make sure that I focused and got accepted on a scholarship to college. Because neither of them could afford the cost of my tuition.

"Wait, is that why you and Luca are fighting? Is it about Zeke?" Kensley doesn't miss a beat.

"Yeah," I say and glance at Ashton, hoping he'll confirm the story for Kensley, because her learning about the mafia is clearly off-limits.

Ashton folds his arms across his chest. "He was pissed you lied to him."

He's still upset, but I don't bother to mention that to Kensley or Ashton.

Because if he hates me forever, our upcoming wedding will never happen. And when it does, it won't make the least bit of sense to anyone.

"And he's forgiven me," I say.

But I'm not sure that he has forgiven me completely.

Ashton's eyes flicker, like he knows that I'm lying, but he doesn't say anything aloud.

Luca has been civil to me when we're in class. We're returned to our study dates for economics, so that I can keep up my grades up for my scholarship, but the quiet moments that we shared, they don't seem to be there anymore.

Except when we're both stuck pretending.

And I could live with that if I have to, because at least pretending with Luca is better than anything happening to Zeke.

Those threats from the Ricci family still linger and scare me. I can't help but glance over my shoulder when I'm alone at night, wondering if someone will jump out of the shadows and grab me. Hurt me.

But the real fear comes from what I can't see or do anything about.

Zeke is with my mother, and I can't protect him while he's not with me.

Maybe bringing him on campus next semester is the best option, because at least I'll be able to look after him and make sure he's safe.

─────────

Kensley and I arrive early to the Narwhals' home game. We're both sporting jerseys for the team and seated in the front row.

I'm doing this for *him*.

I want Luca to realize how much I truly care about him, and that means attending his games.

At least tonight, there's no sign of Quinn, and pretty soon, I won't have to deal with her at all. I look forward to moving in with the boys, and while I know it won't be easy, at least Nova will be there too.

I spent the week finding out about the daycare on campus and how it's open to students during class hours, which is great. I signed up Zeke to enroll next semester while I'm in class and studying.

"Go, Ashton!" Kensley shouts as he snatches the puck from the Wolverines.

I glance at her, curious if she's crushing on him. "Ashton?"

"He's your boyfriend's best friend," she says beside me and stands, shouting and cheering when he knocks another guy into the wall.

Now, she makes me look bad.

Luca catches sight of us, and as quickly as his eyes land on me, they're back on the ice, following the puck, chasing after it. As swiftly as he snatches it from the Wolverines, they knock it away from him.

It's a long game, with zero score in the first period and lots of racing back and forth on the ice, chasing the puck.

The buzzer sounds for the end of the first period, and as the guys start skating off the ice toward the locker room, Luca strolls up to the plexiglass and gives me a wave.

"You came," he says, breathing heavily. He's covered in sweat and glances at his buddies, a few are waiting for him.

"I wanted to support you," I say. It's true, he deserves that much. It sucks knowing his father disapproves of his choice to play hockey. If we're getting married, I want him to realize that I'll always support his decisions, no matter what.

"I'm glad you're here. Maybe you'll be my good luck charm." He offers a crooked grin and then hurries off the ice with the rest of teammates waiting around.

"See, aren't you glad you bought a Narwhals jersey?" Kensley asks, nudging me. "Now you have something to wear at every game."

"Every game," I repeat. I hadn't really thought about attending all of his games, but it would be fun, especially with Zeke. I'd have to get Zeke those cute baby headphones to block out the noise from the crowd, but I'll bet he'd love to watch Luca play hockey.

The players return onto the ice, and Luca is unstoppable. He manages to steal the puck and races down to the goal without almost anyone on him.

He shoots and scores.

Excitement bubbles through the arena as he turns to look at me.

I'm on my feet clapping and cheering, wanting him to know that I'm his biggest fan.

"Louder," Kensley chides into my ear. "He can't hear you."

She's probably right, but I feel like I'm already screaming over the crowd.

———

The Narwhals beat the Wolverines, and as the game ends, Luca skates over to us. "Wait for us. We'll be done in thirty."

"Okay, sure."

He skates to the locker room, and Kensley and I hang out while the fans begin to disperse.

It takes closer to an hour for Luca to return, but he's beaming with excitement, and I'm incredibly happy for him. He comes out of the locker room but wanders through the stands, making his way to our aisle.

"You did great!" I say as he throws his arms around me. He pulls me into a hug, and for a moment, I can't tell if he's happy to see me or this is all an act because we're being forced to marry.

For me, it's never an act.

"Thanks. I'm really glad you showed up tonight. Thanks for bringing her," he says to Kensley.

"It was all Harper's idea," Kensley says. "But I may have had something to do with these." She points at our Narwhal's jerseys.

Luca pulls me close against him, his breath mingling with mine before he goes in for the kill. His lips taste sweet and smell uniquely of sandalwood and amber. His hair is still damp from the recent shower, and a few drops find their way onto my skin.

I lean into him, my tongue seeking entrance into his mouth, momentarily forgetting that Kensley is standing beside us, and the world seems to melt away.

His fingers clench my jersey, keeping me tight and close. I swear I can feel his heart drumming through his chest.

Kensley clears her throat. "Should I just head home?" she asks.

I don't want to break apart the kiss because I don't know when Luca will kiss me again, touch me like he actually means it.

And I don't know whether he means it. I suspect he's *faking* our relationship in the same way he *faked* it with our parents.

There are feelings involved. I know he still cares for me, but he's grown more distant lately, and it hurts me to wonder if I'll ever truly have his heart.

"No," Luca rasps, his breathing heavy as he pulls back from the kiss, ending our tirade.

I wish it had lasted longer. I could go all night just kissing him.

"The guys are meeting up at the house after the game. You're welcome to join us, Kensley," he says and takes my hand, intertwining our fingers together.

He brings our joined hands up to his lips, kissing my palm. Butterflies flutter inside my stomach, and I lean on my tiptoes, stealing another taste of his lips.

Because with Luca, one kiss isn't enough. I've been craving him since the night we fell into bed together, weeks ago.

But those couple of weeks feel like months, years ago even, as I feel the urge to climb into bed with him again.

He smiles and kisses my cheek. "Are you girls riding with me?"

"If you've got room for both of us," Kensley says.

"There's always room for the love of my life and her best friend."

He's still acting, and damn, my heart falls for it every time.

———

Heading into his house, most of his teammates are celebrating the win. There's beer being passed around, and Ashton is on the couch with Nova.

"Don't let her drink!" Luca points at Nova.

"Oh, come on, I'm the same age as Harper now. You can't boss me around anymore."

"You're still under twenty-one. Don't you have school tomorrow?" Luca glares at her.

"Teacher institute day, whatever that means. I get the day off. Dad knows I'm crashing with you."

"Wonderful," Luca answers cooly. "I'm going to grab us drinks, be right back." He drops a quick kiss on my cheek and hurries away.

He's probably glad to get rid of me for a while. I anticipate he'll be gone longer than just a few minutes.

Kensley nudges me and whispers in my ear. "Do you know who that girl is?"

"His little sister," I say. Knowing who she is, there's no longer any jealousy on my part. Turns out she's fun to hang out with.

"Harper!" Nova's eyes widen and she hurries off the sofa, coming over toward me. She throws her arms around me in a huge embrace.

I kind of have to admit that it feels nice. And the best part is it's genuine, unlike Luca's affection toward me.

I introduce Nova and Kensley. "Nova will be joining us next semester on campus," I say.

"That's great," Kensley says. "Do you know what dorm you're moving into yet?"

"No dorm. Luca's mom pulled some strings, and we get to move into a property on campus, some house across town."

"What?" Kensley glances at me. "You didn't mention that you were ditching Quinn. How could you have forgotten to tell me that?"

I laugh under my breath. "I mentioned Zeke living with me, it's not going to be in the dorms."

"Oh, right." Kensley pauses and nods. Her attention is back on Nova. "So, are you and Ashton—"

Does Kensley have a crush on Ashton?

Nova glances back at him on the couch and smiles. There's something there —a smile that I hadn't seen before. "We're not, we're just friends, but I mean, he's

Ashton Rinaldi," she says with so much conviction that it's hard to ignore.

"Got it," Kensley says with a smile. "You like him."

Her eyes widen in horror. "Shh! You can't go saying stuff like that around here. You'll get Luca riled up—"

"Sorry!" Kensley is quick to apologize. "I won't say anything. Promise." She locks her lips and pretends to throw away the key.

"Thanks," Nova says and exhales heavily. She glances back at Ashton, and there's definitely something that crosses her features.

Longing?

Desire?

Did something happen between the two of them?

Ashton has never mentioned it, but from what I've heard from Luca, he sleeps his way through campus, especially the freshman class and any girls who flirt with him about hockey.

But he never sleeps with the same girl twice, which has me worried for Nova.

If she actually likes him, I don't want her to get her heart broken.

"Just be careful with him," I say, keeping my voice low.

Over the crowd, it's doubtful anyone else hears me, and I can tell that Nova is struggling to hear my warning.

"You don't have to worry about me. Gosh, you and Luca are so much alike," Nova says with a nervous laugh. "Are you going to be my next big, great protector? And to think I was about to ask you how you're doing and tell you that I missed you this weekend."

"I'm good, and I missed you too." It would have made dinner a hell of a lot easier had Nova and her parents been there. Perhaps they could have been the buffer that we desperately needed.

I pull her in for another hug and whisper into her ear, "I need someone in my corner." Nova is the only one I can undoubtedly trust.

Not that I don't trust Kensley—she's my best friend —but I can't go telling her about what happened at Luca's parents' house.

I can't speak of the missing little boy who I found locked in the basement or that his parents are mafia.

At least Nova knows all of it. She's someone I can confide in and trust that she won't get me killed.

At least, I don't think that she has any reason to hate me.

Nova pulls back and smiles genuinely. She squeezes my arm. "You've got me, sis. I'm not going anywhere."

Kensley watches with rapt curiosity, and then Luca saunters back, two beers in hand, offering me one.

"You offer Harper a beer but not me? We're the same age, jackass." Nova glares at Luca, and I swear she's about ready to start a fight with him.

I hand her my beer. "Take it."

"Harper!" Luca growls at me, and I shove her toward the sofa. "Go hang out with Ashton; keep him company. He looks lonely."

Nova willingly takes the beer bottle but pretends to glare at Ashton and then back at me. "Seriously? Like I don't see enough of him all evening."

But from the looks and the conversation earlier, I genuinely suspect she's as good at faking not liking Ashton as Luca is as good at faking liking me.

Luca is still scowling at me. "I can't believe you gave her that beer."

"Well, you don't have to worry for much longer," I say.

"Why's that?" he asks and steps closer, invading my personal space. He brushes a strand of hair out of my eyes.

"Next semester, Nova and I will be living here, with Zeke."

He watches me for a moment, the realization dawning on him. His life is about to change.

"We'll just find somewhere else to celebrate after a win," Luca says, but there's something else behind his stare that I can't quite chase.

Kensley glances at Luca. "Any of your friends single?" she asks.

He laughs under his breath. "Sure, but it depends. Are you looking for a fling or a relationship?"

"I don't need to get married," she says, staring at Luca, and I feel like she's taking a jab, but I'm not sure why. Kensley has been supportive one hundred percent with me about the engagement and finding out I have a son.

He laughs darkly and sips his beer. "Ashton's only interested in a one-night hookup." He points at his other roommate, whom I've barely seen around the house. "Liam is more into friends-with-benefits, from what I hear. Then there's Chase, who is recently single, and I'd guess it'll be rebound sex. He's still quite hung up on his ex."

Kensley glances at the guys Luca pointed out and then back at me. "I think you lucked out and picked a good one." She pats my arm. "I'm going to mingle."

"Sure," I say and smile, watching her wander off into the crowd. I don't know how she does it. I hate big crowds. The house right now feels overwhelming, but with Luca by my side, I'm at least feeling a bit better.

"How are you doing?" he asks, his lips brushing against my ear.

"Okay."

He stares at me, waiting for a real answer, it seems.

"You know I'm not big on parties," I confess.

"Do you want to go upstairs, hang out, just the two of us?" Luca asks.

Silently, I nod, and he takes my hand and whisks me upstairs to his bedroom. Stepping inside, he closes the door behind us, and the chatter and loudness seem to dissipate behind the closed door.

While I can still hear the commotion, it's muffled.

My heartbeat slows to a steady rhythm. I hadn't realized it was racing. "Can I sit?" I ask, gesturing to his bed.

"It's your room too," he says. "It will be soon enough."

My mouth parts, and a soft sigh slips past. I hadn't even considered that we'd be *sharing* a bedroom together.

"What?"

"I just thought that we'd have our own rooms in the new place."

Luca's eyes shine, but there's no smile on his face. He steps closer and guides me to sit on the bed beside him. Maybe having some time alone, just the two of us, is a good idea.

We still have so much to talk about, and I feel like I barely see him anymore. At least, I don't see him when it's just the two of us, where we can talk freely.

"Your son, Zeke, will have a bedroom. Unless you'd rather share with him and we can sleep in separate rooms. Our marriage is for show, and anyone living under our roof already knows the truth about our relationship."

"I just, I didn't think you'd want to share a bed with me," I whisper.

The only time he's shown any affection has been when he's been forced to because someone is watching and he's putting on an act.

He reaches for my hand, taking it between his palms. "I do care deeply for you, Harper. Please don't think my feelings aren't real. I wouldn't have done this, suggested the marriage, if I didn't care about you."

"I know," I whisper, realizing this doesn't just weigh heavily on me. It's a burden that he's forced to carry as well. My heart hurts, my stomach is in knots, and I stare down at my lap, not wanting him to see the pain etched all over my face. "I'm sorry."

Tears trickle down my cheek, and I release my grip on his hand, wiping them away.

This isn't how I thought my life would go.

Zeke was a surprise.

It had been an emotional rollercoaster, but I felt like I'd finally got back on track, and now, I'm spinning off course all over again.

Luca wraps his arms around my shoulders, pulling me against him. His embrace is warm, firm, his breath tickles my neck as he holds me tight.

"Every day we spend together, I fall more in love with you," I whisper between tears.

I'm met with his silence.

Which only leads to more tears that cascade like a waterfall, and as quickly as I try to hide them, they keep coming.

But he continues to hold me, not the least bit

languishing in his tight grip. Instead, he pulls me onto his lap.

"I've got you," he says, and his cheek brushes mine.

His skin is warm, and his touch draws me closer. I shift slightly, tilting my head up, our breaths mingling together.

I want to kiss him. I crave feeling his body against mine, every inch of him naked, but I fear that he'll pull away from me as he's done the past two weeks.

"Harper," he moans my name as our lips haven't so much as touched yet. But just the sound is enough to stir all of my senses.

I thread my fingers through his hair, closing the gap slowly, effortlessly as I drink him in. His mouth against mine is like fire, and I can't get enough.

His hands roam over my body. One hand presses against my hip, holding me against him, keeping me firmly planted on his lap.

The pads of his fingers graze the hem of my shirt, finding bare skin as he inches the material up just slightly, his touch teasing the waistband of my jeans.

My lips are fused with his; heated kisses aren't nearly enough.

I want him.

Need him.

His one hand remains on my hip, the other caresses my cheek, opening my mouth, deepening the kiss.

My need is matched only by his.

Desire blends with necessity as he drags me backward, farther onto the mattress and lies down, letting me lie above him.

He keeps one arm snaked around my hip, not letting me out of his grip.

I shift only slightly to fully straddle his hips, and Luca groans as I grind against him.

"If you don't want to take things all the way tonight, then we need to stop right now," Luca growls.

He's trying to be a gentleman.

Fuck, I've been wanting him since the night I crawled into his bed, and I haven't stopped wanting him, not once.

I shift only slightly so that I move my hands to my waist to remove the jersey.

"Leave that on," Luca says and smiles up at me. "I like seeing you in my jersey. I'm going to fuck you in it if you'll have me."

My pussy clenches at his words, and my lips capture his. I work the button on my jeans free, unzipping them hastily and kicking them to the floor.

Clad in my panties and the Narwhals jersey, I grind against his hips, feeling what it's doing to him.

"You're going to kill me," he groans.

I place a kiss on his lips and then move down his neck. I lift his t-shirt slowly, drawing a soft pattern of warm kisses and light touches across his chest as I help him disrobe.

He moans beneath my touch, his body responding to every caress of bare skin as I get him down to solely his boxers.

He flips me over, taking control, his hands moving from my hips up under my jersey. "You're still wearing too many clothes." He notices my bra and pinches the clasp.

He shifts off me long enough for me to remove my bra while he tosses his boxers at the door and then he climbs down my body, his fingers hooking the waistband of my panties and guiding them down my thighs.

"Have you been a good girl for me?" Luca asks, staring down at me, straight into my soul.

I roll my lips together, unsure of what he's asking.

"Have you touched yourself since I made you come?" Luca asks.

My eyes widen, and my breath catches in my throat.

"You have, haven't you? When you're my wife, the only one who will be making you come is *me*."

I whimper, and my head lolls back as his breath tickles my inner thighs. He's fucking teasing me and enjoying it.

"Do you want me to touch you?"

"Yes," I whisper, my fingers tangling in his hair.

He chuckles and kisses my thighs and inches closer to my heated center, but he's taking his sweet ass time.

"You're killing me," I groan, growing restless.

"Then beg me," he says, his gray eyes tearing into mine. "Are you going to beg me to fuck you with my tongue?"

His breath tickles my pussy lips as he lets his lips trail closer, and I lean upward into him.

"Not yet," he commands. "You haven't begged me for what you want."

"I want to feel your tongue on me." My voice is raspy; it betrays me as I'm already gasping for air, my heart racing, and he's barely touched me.

"Good girl," he whispers, and his mouth descends on my pussy. His tongue teases me, flicks and licks, his hands hold my hips, keeping me against him as I already begin to tremble.

My eyes close and my lips part, already feeling the warmth spreading through my body.

"Eyes on me, baby," Luca says, and I struggle to meet his stare.

"I like when you listen to me." A grin spreads across his face and his mouth descends once again, bringing me right to the edge before he pulls away.

"Asshole," I mutter, and he chuckles.

"You're so fucking hot when you're turned on and frustrated," Luca says.

I throw up my middle finger at him, and he pounces on me, pinning me down, binding my hands with his grip.

"You're so incredibly sexy," he says, and I feel my body melt from his words alone. "Let's see how ready you are for me."

His fingers tease my folds, slipping one finger in as he curls it, and I shift slightly, finding that sweet spot.

Through heavy-lidded eyes, I stare up at him, but the struggle is real, and I let my eyes fall shut.

"Did you just purr?" Luca whispers into my ear as a soft moan spills past my lips. "God, that's fucking hot."

His mouth is on mine as he guides two thick fingers inside of me, stroking me.

His touch is like fire, sending sparks coursing through me as heat floods my entire body, and as he pushes a third finger inside, my walls clench down, feeling the ripple of my first orgasm descending on me.

He keeps stroking me with his fingers, curling them inside as his lips capture my mouth. His tongue pushes past my lips as I rise, my back arching into him as I chase the wave before it comes crashing down.

My heart slams against my chest, my body trembling in his grasp, as I moan and shudder, finally letting go.

It takes a few seconds for me to catch my breath, and Luca releases his hold on me.

"I love watching you come for me," Luca says, kissing my lips as I nibble on his bottom lip with a wry smile.

"I want to taste you," I say, moving down his body, rolling us around so that he's on his back. I move down his body, my breath teasing over the head before my tongue swipes out to touch him. I leave a trail of kisses down his length, listening to each sound he makes, memorizing all of them.

With each stroke of my tongue, his breathing quickens. I let my fingers graze over the shaft, my touch soft yet firm as I bring him farther in past my lips.

"Fuck, Harper." He moans, and his fingers tangle in my hair, tugging me away. "Not like this," he mutters.

"You don't want me to let you finish?" I ask, staring up at him, breathing heavy as he drags me back onto the bed on my back.

"You're such a good fucking girl for me, but I want your pussy to swallow me," he rasps into my ear. "I'd rather feel you wrapped around my cock."

He pins me down against the bed, and I hate to admit I love the feeling of him dominating me. It's new for me, letting someone else be in control, and Luca definitely checks all those boxes.

He reaches for the bedside table and retrieves a condom, sheathing it over his cock and poising himself at my entrance.

"You're so sexy, Harper." He stares down at me, one hand sliding up beneath the jersey, caressing my breast, while his other hand stays firmly planted on his cock.

He rubs the head over my pussy, making me antsy and restless.

I move my hips, trying to bring him closer and guide him inside of me, but he'd rather take his time and drag every second out to eternity.

Sweet fucking torture.

"I want you to fuck me, Luca," I moan. "Please." I sound desperate, but I feel even needier than I've ever felt in my life.

I'm clearly not above begging.

If that's what it'll take to get him to give me want I crave—his cock—then so be it.

"Good girl," he whispers and covers my lips with his. "I like it when you beg me."

But he's still not driving his cock inside of me yet.

"Are you going to fuck me or talk about it?" I gasp, already breathless with need, and frustration begins mounting.

He chuckles as he guides his thick cock inside of me.

"Look how well you're taking me," he rasps into my ear and tugs the lobe between his teeth.

He moves with me, his hips pounding against mine with each thrust, and I'm clawing at his back, craving even more contact with him.

I take him deeper, bringing my legs around him, not letting him go as I match his movements, grinding against him.

"Keep doing that," he growls, and I watch as euphoria clouds his features. He struggles to keep his eyes on me, his arms at either side as he keeps his momentum going, and he's teetering on the edge.

"Fuck, you feel so good," he gasps, and I can see the struggle as his body grows closer.

I clench onto his cock, squeezing down as the orgasm begins rippling through me, and heat floods my senses.

"Come with me," I whisper into his ear, my tongue teasing the sensitive spot on his neck that seems to rile him up. "I'm so close, Luca."

"You're going to kill me," he pants, and I know he's close too. He moans, and his breaths and the feel of him inside me are enough to send me over into oblivion again.

I don't have to tell him I'm coming. My back arches off the mattress, my toes curling, the moan rips through me as my hands claw at his back and down to his ass, bringing him closer, tighter, needing to feel him buried as deep as possible within me.

And it's only then that I feel Luca letting go. His body trembles and tightens, gasping for breath as he finally collapses above me.

After, he pulls me against him, the condom discarded and the lights turned off. There's still music pulsating through the walls because the party hasn't died down yet, but none of it matters.

It's just the two of us together, in our own little world.

Luca's arm holds me close as my back is nestled against him.

His slow, even breaths caress my neck as we lie together in bed. "Shit," he mumbles against my neck and drops a lazy kiss over my bare skin.

"What's wrong?" I ask, turning slightly to glance back at him.

He holds me tighter.

"Nova is downstairs. She's going to need a bed for tonight. Usually, I let her crash in here and I take the couch."

He rolls onto his back, and I shift around, draping a leg over his hips. "She can take the couch," I say.

"Yeah, but if any of the guys stay over, I don't want them pawing her or making her uncomfortable."

He's quiet for a moment, and I can't help but think that he's fallen asleep.

"Ashton knows how I feel about Nova staying here during parties. He's a good friend. I'm sure he'll offer his bed to sleep in."

SEVEN

NOVA

The beer that Harper gave me is absolutely disgusting. No wonder she offered it to me. It tastes like piss.

Not that I've ever drank urine, I'm just assuming that's what it tastes like because it's so incredibly awful.

I grab a bottle of water and crash on the sofa next to Ashton.

"No hot hookup tonight?" I ask.

I'm well aware that he's got player status written all over him.

"Do you see a lot of hot girls here?" Ashton asks.

I glance around and know he's right. The party was a last-minute get-together. Thrown exclusively because they won by a landslide.

Had they lost, the guys would be sitting at home commiserating on their own.

"I mean, there's the girl over there," I say and nod, trying not to gesture and point her out.

She's a redhead, cute, but dressed a little unflattering, not that the guys probably care much for a girl's style. But she's talking to Chase, another one of the Narwhals' players.

"Yeah, I think Chase has first dibs on her."

"I'm happy to keep you company," I say and shrug like I don't mind being his hangout buddy for the evening.

I mean, that's not exactly what I want in regard to Ashton, but I've got to play this carefully. I'm going to be living with him in a couple of weeks. The last thing we want is a messy situationship.

I've done my best to temper those thoughts, especially from my older brother. The last thing I need is for Luca to cockblock me and force me to live in the dorms my first semester.

Maybe pining for Ashton is a bad idea, but fuck, it's Ashton Rinaldi and he's gorgeous. It's hard not to imagine what he'd look like naked.

And I've seen him shirtless.

He's one hell of a specimen.

Pretty sure he knows it too. Probably why he manages to sleep his way through Evergreen.

"You're staring at me. Do I have a booger coming out of my nose?" He swipes at his face, and I playfully shove him.

"That's gross, and you're perfect. I mean, you look perfect. You're fine. I'm just going to shut up now."

Shit.

I blame the couple sips of piss beer for my loose lips.

Ashton offers me his wayward grin, and his nose crinkles just slightly.

Holy hell, it's rare to see that smile.

"If I didn't know any better, I'd say you have a crush on me."

Fuck me.

"In your dreams, Ashton," I say, denying it.

He can't know.

I mean, I like him. I want him, but this—whatever it is between us that's been slowly evolving can't happen.

Luca would kill Ashton.

"You've crossed a few of my dreams," Ashton says and takes another swig of beer.

Oh shit. Did he really just say that he dreams about me?

Is he messing with me? It seems like something a friend of Luca's would do.

But this is Ashton, he's not just any friend or roommate to Luca. I've been hanging around Ashton for months. Hell, he even let me give him a colorful manicure without so much as batting an eye.

Not even my brother was that willing to appease me.

"Your dreams?" I repeat, my breath catching in my throat. I don't even know how to answer because it's Ashton, and he's this ever-evolving crush that I can't seem to escape, nor do I want to.

Ashton stretches and rests his arms on the back of the sofa.

I've seen that maneuver in movies, when a guy wants to wrap an arm around a girl's shoulder.

Is he being coy or fucking with me?

I honestly can't tell, and I take another swig of the disgusting piss drink just to gather a little more courage.

Unfortunately, it isn't an instant drink-and-be-brave potion.

"You don't want to hear about my dreams," Ashton says and throws me a wink.

My body heats and I shift on the sofa to face him.

"Are you flirting with me, Ashton?"

His eyes tighten, and he smiles lazily. "Would it be so bad if I did, Nova?"

It's the way he says my name that sends tingles down to my core.

Ashton leans closer, his lips brushing my ear. "I can't stop thinking about you. You invade all of my thoughts, my dreams. I want to kiss you."

My mouth parts and I stare at him in disbelief. If this is a game, it's cruel.

"You want to kiss me?" My voice betrays me as my mouth grows dry. Holy hell, I never thought a guy could make my insides heat from just a simple phrase of the tongue.

His thumb grazes my cheek, his hand on my jaw, guiding his lips to mine. "Tell me to stop if you don't want me, Nova."

It's that voice that's toe-curling when he whispers my name. Maybe it's just because I've got it bad for Ashton Rinaldi.

His lips move closer, hovering over mine, his breath mingling with my own as he pauses, waiting for me to either make the next move and lean in or pull away.

His gentle caress against my cheek pulls me in, finding his lips against mine. The kiss is soft and sweet at first, gentle and inviting.

I don't want it to end, and I pull him against me, tasting beer and something else distinctly Ashton.

He smells incredible. He showered after the game, and the fresh scent still lingers like cologne and mixed with a woodsy soap that tickles my senses.

It is uniquely Ashton, and I could drink it in forever.

Our lips tangle, and his fingers move to the base of my neck, holding me tight, bringing me closer.

I feel the need stirring and climb onto his lap, straddling him.

His mouth is fused on mine, my hands caress across his back, holding him close, needing to feel one with him.

Ashton pulls back, both of us gasping for air. He rests his forehead against mine as he stares straight into my soul.

"You should sit back down on the sofa if you don't want this going any farther," Ashton says.

My heart is racing as I try to catch my breath.

"I want you," I whisper, feeling the courage to tell him exactly how I feel.

He moans and covers my lips with his again.

This time, the kiss is even more intense, his tongue pushing its way past my mouth as he lays me down on the sofa and climbs above me.

His weight makes me feel safe, comforted as he peppers kisses across my jaw and back up to my lips.

"We can't do this down here," I whisper, staring up at him with a laugh.

It isn't just the two of us in this room. His housemates and teammates are watching. Although most seem preoccupied. It's not the first time; I'm sure they've seen two people making out.

But a few sets of eyes are on us, Liam's glaring, and I can't help but worry that he might tell Luca.

Any of them could.

"Take me upstairs to bed," I say, wanting Ashton to show me to his room.

He lifts me into his arms with ease. "Don't have to tell me twice." He manhandles me to the staircase.

I smack his chest. "Put me down this instant!" The last thing I want is to go tumbling down because he's showing off in front of his buddies.

"Fine," Ashton grumbles and sets my feet onto the ground, his hands at my waist as his fingers kiss my skin beneath my clothes.

His touch is overwhelming, and I wrap my arms around his neck, taking another taste. "Lead the way," I mumble between kisses.

He takes my hand and guides me upstairs.

I've crashed in Luca's room in the past, but I've never stayed in Ashton's bedroom.

Quietly, we pass by my brother's room and hurry to Ashton's room. He opens the door, flips on the light, and gestures for me to step inside first.

There's a hamper in the corner of the room, a few dirty clothes hanging off it that were clearly tossed in and didn't quite make it inside.

His dresser has folded clothes on top that haven't

been put away, but it's not as terrible as I thought it'd be.

There are no food wrappers or empty pizza boxes lying on the floor.

The room smells like him but fresher, like a forest of oak and evergreens. I notice a candle in the corner of his room.

"So, this is your room," I say, taking it all in.

"Not what you were expecting?" He closes the door and locks it, giving us an ample amount of privacy.

"With the way Luca talks about you being messy, I kind of expected a disaster zone," I confess. "It's not bad."

Ashton smirks and comes to sit at the edge of the mattress. "Luca likes to exaggerate."

I laugh under my breath and stride the remaining distance, wanting to feel him beneath my touch.

"If we do this, Luca can't know," I say.

"You want me to keep a secret from my best friend?" Ashton rests his hands on the bed at his sides and leans back.

There's a genuine smirk that crosses his face.

"What?" I ask.

"Wouldn't be the first secret I've kept from him."

"Care to elaborate?" I swear he knows how to have me hanging on the edge. I climb onto his lap, straddling him again, this time grateful for the privacy.

"No, then it wouldn't be a secret," Ashton says. He leans in, his breath tickling my neck, leaving a trail of kisses before he finds that super sensitive spot that has me wriggling my hips over his.

His hands steady my waist with a soft chuckle. His lips pause over my neck, and he lifts his head, meeting my stare. "I need to know something, and be honest with me, Nova."

"Always." I don't have any reason to lie to him or hide anything. He knows about my family, who they are, what they do. I know about his father running the Chicago mafia.

We're not so different, the two of us.

And there aren't any big secrets between us.

I can live with keeping a secret from my brother.

"Are you a virgin?" Ashton asks.

"Yes, but that doesn't change that I know what I want," I say.

His gaze hardens for a brief moment. He's hesitating, and I hate that my honesty is causing that.

"I should have told you I wasn't as, clearly, it bothers you."

Ashton holds my jaw, his stare never wavering. "Don't ever lie to me."

"I didn't, but you're either thinking I'm untouchable or pathetic. I'm not sure which."

Ashton guides me onto my back, lying down beside me on the mattress. His hand remains on my hip, keeping me close to him.

"You're not pathetic," his voice heavy and thick.

"So, I'm untouchable," I mutter and pull to roll away and climb out of bed, but he keeps a firm hold on me, bringing me closer against him.

"Your emotions are fragile." He brushes a strand of hair behind my ear, and I lean into his touch.

"I'm not going to break, Ashton. I know your reputation. You sleep with a girl once and then you move on."

His eyes flicker, and he frowns. "Is that all you want? One night?"

I'm not stupid to think that he'd give me more than that. "I'll take what I can get with the hottest player on the Narwhals." I smirk, and he pulls away.

"What'd I say?" I sit up in bed, confused. "I've seen the girls you bed. I've heard things from Luca. You don't do relationships. I'm telling you I'm okay with that."

"You say that now, but I know you're not."

Why is he second-guessing what I'm saying? "Is this because I've never had sex with a guy? "I've done other stuff..." I say and trail off. "Just because I haven't had a dick in me, it doesn't mean I'm going to fall in love with the first guy who fucks me."

He laughs darkly.

"What's so funny?" I sit up in bed, scooting to the edge, and Ashton is right there beside me.

"Let's not fight," he says.

"You're the one telling me you know me better than I know myself." I stand, needing some space. It's crazy how much the one guy I have feelings for has the ability to turn me on and make me hate him at the same time.

Except, I don't actually hate him.

I'm just really angry with him for making decisions without me.

"If you're not going to be my first, I'll find someone else downstairs who's willing to have sex with me." I'm egging him on. If he won't be reasonable, then I guess that means he'll be miserable tonight.

Makes two of us.

I glare at him as I head for his bedroom door.

"Chase just broke up with his girlfriend. I'm sure he'd be excited to get back in the sack for rebound sex," I say.

"You're not fucking Chase Lancaster," Ashton growls at me.

"If he's not interested, there's Liam, your other roommate," I say. "I hear he's into friends-with-benefits, and I could really use a friend right now."

Ashton throws his arms into the air.

"For fuck's sake, Nova, I am your friend!" He leaps off the bed and blocks me from leaving. He grabs my arm, spinning me around. "If you want me to fuck you, just say so."

"I've been saying that!" I shout at him, and his mouth is on me, hard, fast, furious.

It's rough and exhilarating.

He claws at my Narwhals jersey and yanks it forcefully over my head. He tosses it across the room and lifts me into his arms.

My legs wrap around his waist as he carries me to the bed and lays me down against the mattress.

His mouth is on me, and as he kisses a path down my neck, over that sensitive bit of flesh; he nips it and I moan.

Ashton chuckles, and his hands work my pants down. "Lift your hips," he mumbles against my neck, helping me out of my clothes as he kisses his way down my body.

Clad in panties and a bra, I scoot back on the

mattress while Ashton quickly disrobes, leaving absolutely nothing on.

My eyes don't seem to leave his cock, admiring the sight of it.

"First time seeing one in the flesh?" he asks, a cheeky grin on his face.

"I've done stuff with my high school boyfriend," I say.

"You broke up with him last year?" Ashton asks, clearly remembering me telling him about it.

"Yes."

Ashton's kisses are soft and warm, peppering his way across my chest, focusing on my breasts. "Tell me what you liked and what you didn't."

"Oral," I say as he kisses my bra straps down and then unfastens the clasp, removing me of the undergarment.

"Love it or hate it?" Ashton asks. His mouth moves across my breast, his tongue flicking over my nipple, and I arch into him.

Fuck, he knows what he's doing. Can't say the same for that high school ex.

"Didn't particularly love it," I confess. "Just felt really wet and odd."

Ashton's lips move across my stomach and to my navel. My stomach flutters as he drops soft butterfly kisses across my skin and his fingers hook into my panties, sliding them down my thighs.

"Would you be willing to try it again? Or is it a hard no?" Ashton asks.

"Once," I say, raising an eyebrow at him. "But you don't have to—I thought we were having sex."

He smiles and lifts my hips, guiding my legs over his shoulders. "Baby, we are. I'm just getting started."

My pulse quickens as his breath tickles and nuzzles my pussy, the anticipation a sweet type of agony that I can't say I've ever felt.

It might also be his confidence, making me a bit more comfortable.

Ashton kisses and licks my folds, using his tongue to fuck me while he slowly guides his ministrations up along my clit. But he doesn't touch it. He goes everywhere the fuck around it with his tongue, swirling and making a pattern as he taps and licks, sucks and grazes the one spot that craves contact.

My hands bunch at the bedsheets, tangling between my fingers, clenching as he caresses that sweet perfect spot and works me into a tizzy.

My legs begin to tremble and my body quakes as heat roars through me.

"Come for me, baby," Ashton mumbles and continues his pace, bringing me flying over the edge as wetness seeps out of me and he licks every last drop.

"Verdict?" he asks, not the least bit concerned about how I'll answer.

"That's what it's supposed to feel like?" I rasp, sitting up in bed, trying to catch my breath as Ashton leans in and kisses me.

"You've never had an orgasm before?" he guesses.

I blush and glance away nervously.

Ashton guides my chin up to meet his stare. His eyes shine. "Don't ever hide from me," he says with such conviction, my breath catches in my throat.

"Never," I whisper.

"And you're absolutely adorable when you come."

"Now it's your turn." I smirk and push him onto his back, straddling him.

"We are not doing cowgirl for your first time," Ashton says.

My eyes narrow, wondering why the hell not, but that wasn't what I was intending. "I want to try to get you off with my tongue. Will you—guide me?" I ask.

I'm not nearly as skilled as Ashton is in oral, but I want him to feel amazing.

My kisses move lower across his chest and down his abdomen.

Ashton groans and rests his hands on my shoulders. "I want to say yes, but if you wrap your tongue around my cock, I don't think I'll be able to stop you tonight. Let's just focus on you."

"Quit being a gentleman; it's so unlike you," I grumble at him, and he laughs.

"A gentleman would buy you dinner before taking you to bed," Ashton says, and then his brow pinches.

I glare at him. "If you so much as think of stopping, I'll end you."

He smiles and leans in, his lips brushing against mine. "Wouldn't dream of it." He rolls us around on the bed, putting me on my back, his lips on my neck and his fingers between my thighs, teasing my folds apart.

I glide my hand across his stomach and then lower, grazing the head of his cock with my thumb. "You can't tell me you're ready yet," I argue with him and wrestle Ashton onto his back, wanting control.

"You're not going down on me, Nova," he growls.

"Wouldn't dream of it," I mock him with his own words.

Ashton snarls at me, but I know it's all playful—at least I think it is—until he whips us around and tackles me again on my back.

His mouth descends on mine, silencing me before I have time to object.

His hands press my hands into the mattress, intertwining our fingers together.

Those lips. His kisses.

My insides melt, and all thoughts of dominating him float away.

He grinds against my hips, and damn, do I feel ready to come undone all over again.

One hand relinquishes its grip as he guides his fingers across my hip, his touch tantalizing and burning a trail like hot embers over my skin.

The room swelters as my body heats up once again, solely from his touch.

He nuzzles my neck, his kisses and lips find that spot that has my toes curling from just his breath.

How the hell does he manage to do that?

I whimper and shudder, the heat radiating through me, and I briefly wonder if I might physically burn him.

Ashton's lips suckle on my neck before gliding down to my breasts as he guides one finger into my warmth. "Relax," he whispers against my skin, his mouth moving back up to mine.

"Hard to relax," I mumble through half-lidded eyes as his fingers dance inside my pussy and he guides a second finger into me, stretching me.

"You said *hard*." Ashton grins down at me.

I glare at him, and my silence is met with a searing kiss to my lips. My mouth parts, wanting to taste him.

Our tongues delve together, fighting for control, but I let him lead this one time, because he certainly knows what the hell he's doing.

My body is atingle from his fingers and earlier with his tongue.

I don't know how long I'll last before the next wave surfaces.

"I want to feel you inside of me," I whisper between heated kisses.

Ashton glides a third finger, stretching me, and the pain feels amazing.

My back arches off the mattress, toes curling as I feel close. "Ashton, I'm going to—"

He keeps the same rhythm and pace, his fingers curling inside of my pussy as the first wave assaults me and my body trembles against the mattress.

Our mouths fuse together, my tongue pushing past his lips, craving more, needing him more than anything right now.

It's like watching a firefly in the darkness of a summer's night, and I'm chasing after it, trying to catch it.

"Come for me, Nova," Ashton whispers, and his breath, his voice, the fact I'm actually here, in *his* bed, is enough to draw me over the edge.

Trembling and gasping, my body gives in as I groan his name in ecstasy.

I collapse against the mattress, gasping for breath, trying to draw air into my lungs as my heart pounds wildly against my ribcage.

"You said you'd fuck me," I rasp, glaring at him.

"Sweetheart, we're not done," Ashton says as he grabs a condom and sheaths it before he climbs above me.

I'm glad he was thinking ahead because my brain is in such a haze that I'd have forgotten protection.

Hell, I can barely even remember my own name right now.

His cock is in his hand, stroking his shaft, teasing the folds of my pussy while he stares at me.

"Catch your breath." Ashton stares down at me. "I'm going to need you to be alive for the next part."

I snort and smack his arm.

"What?" He acts offended, but I doubt that he truly is because he's not moving off of me.

"Joking about *that* right now, it's a dick move."

Ashton rolls his eyes. "Lighten up. You're about to have your third orgasm of the night." He beams down proudly; clearly, his ego has already been stroked.

"Just shut up and fuck me already." I glare up at him.

"Oh, listen to all that sexy talk," Ashton mocks. His eyes are shining, clearly loving being in control.

Turns out, I don't actually mind him being on top. I kind of like it, but I'm not ready to tell him that just yet.

He teases me with the head of his cock, stroking my folds but not inching inside of me.

"Tell me again how you want me to fuck you, but say it like you mean it," Ashton commands.

"Fuck me," I say, glaring up at him. "Or I'll get one of the other guys downstairs to do it."

A flash of heat settles on his face. "The fuck you will," he growls at me and inches his cock inside my pussy.

My fingernails grip his shoulder, feeling him stretch my walls, and holy hell, does it ache, but it also feels really incredible.

Ashton's mouth is on mine as he moves all the way inside of me, going deep, and I gasp a loud, "Fuck."

He stops moving, settling himself for a second, but then he just stares down, watching me.

My lips part, staring up with hazy eyes. "Why'd you stop?" He feels so incredible and to be robbed of this would be torture.

He studies my face before dropping a kiss to my lips. "I don't want to hurt you."

"Seriously? You're huge and you just full-on rammed that *thing* into me."

Ashton laughs and rests his forehead against mine. "Okay, I can take it out." He moves his hips back, away from me, and guides his cock out of my pussy.

Already I feel empty, my insides craving more.

"God, you're such an asshole sometimes." I grab his ass, pulling him toward me. "Get back here."

"Can't ever satisfy you, can I?" Aston's smiling down at me, gloating.

He positions himself at my entrance again, but this time, he eases in slowly, and it feels so amazing. His lips graze my ear. "Don't ever threaten to fuck any of my brothers," he growls.

"Or what?" I challenge.

It seems I've discovered Ashton's red flag, or maybe it's just his weakness. Either way, I find it entirely hot that I can aggravate him so easily with just a few simple words.

"I'll fuck you in front of all of them," Ashtons says, biting down on my bottom lip.

My insides quake.

Each thrust gains momentum, and I feel like I'm floating high above the clouds. I try to flip us around, wanting to take control, but Ashton is too strong, and he's moving too hard and fast with his hips to let me gain the upper hand.

"Ashton." My voice betrays me, the sound reverberating like a moan as I clutch him tighter, wanting him deeper.

"That's right, you're going to fucking come a third time for me tonight."

Hearing *that* tone and his voice, it brings me close, but I'm not quite there. I'm not sure I'm even capable of coming a third time in one night.

But the words don't come as I open my lips, and instead, my breaths are soft and filled with moans as his body thrusts and I grind my hips, trying to keep up with him and match his pace.

My back arches, and my hands grip his arms. "I'm so close," I rasp, panting as I'm struggling to keep control.

I wrap a leg around him, pulling him deeper, tighter, trying to keep him against me as my insides tremble.

"Come with me," he whispers into my ear.

My eyes slam shut, the sensations overwhelming as I struggle to breathe, let alone focus on anything other than the amazing way my body feels.

His fingers dive between our bodies, teasing my clit, circling and grazing the still-sensitive bead as he continues thrusting, and holy hell, I am going to explode into a million pieces.

My grip on his forearm tightens, but I don't want to hurt him. I move my hands across his back, down his ass, clawing at him, craving him like a drug, and I need my next hit.

My body arches off the mattress, tightening my grip around him as I tremble and groan, feeling the impending wave coming.

"I'm going to—" I gasp, and Ashton is right there with me, keeping his movements timed for me, knowing what I need as my body gives in and wraps around his cock, squeezing him.

My insides throb as the quivers pulsate through my body, like little tremors, as I clench down and let go.

It's only a few seconds and then Ashton picks up speed, his deliberate strokes that were paced and timed perfectly for me go harder, faster, quicker until I hear his groan and feel his body tense and shudder as he comes right after me.

He's panting hard, sweat dripping from his brow as he rolls off me, discards the condom, before lying with me on his mattress. There's not much room for two, but we make it work.

He curls against me, keeping me close, with his hand over my hip.

He draws lazy patterns across my skin, and I lean back into his embrace, comforted.

"You should know," his warm breath tickles my neck, "I never let anyone spend the night in my room."

A smile spreads across my face as I fight a yawn. "Well, I'm not leaving. So, if you want the room to yourself, then you'd better get out."

Ashton kisses the bare skin of my shoulder. "You're brave, kicking me out of *my* room."

"Don't go pulling the *my daddy is mafia* card." I yawn and let my eyes drift shut. "I have that one too."

"That isn't what I meant."

"Are you sure?" I yawn again.

"Sleep," Ashton says and leans over slightly to drop a kiss on my cheek. "Quit fighting with me."

"Quit keeping me awake," I grumble. "You gave me three orgasms, and I'm exhausted."

He laughs softly. "Yes, boss. Anything else I can do for you, my queen?"

He's mocking me.

"Don't make me wake my brother and have him kick your ass," I threaten.

I'm joking, but he doesn't laugh. Because we both know Luca finding out about what happened is a terrible idea.

EIGHT

LUCA

Friday night, I drive over to my parents' house as planned. We have dinner, all of us, including Moreno, Paige, and Nova tonight.

I'm glad to have Nova around, because she's at least someone under this roof I can trust and count on.

Although she won't be living here for much longer, which is both a relief and a regret. I'm glad she's coming to EU. I'm not thrilled that she'll be moving in with us, because I don't want any of the guys getting any lurid ideas about my sister.

She's off-limits.

I've made it clear that no one touches her, but it was also because she was seventeen and in high school.

Nova is eighteen now, and she starts college in a couple of weeks. It's going to be hard chasing all the boys away from her.

But maybe Harper can help me with that too. Somehow, between her time with Zeke and studying, she can chase the guys away from Nova.

Or maybe just having a baby around the house will chase them away. I mean, who wants the constant reminder of what can happen if you're not playing it safe?

After dinner, Dante corners me in the hallway, alone. "We'll start first thing in the morning with your training," he says.

I have no idea what that will entail. Being stuck with Dante for the weekend, doing whatever dirty job he requires of me is not something I'm looking forward to.

But I know what I signed up for, and I swallow the seeds of doubt and get on with it.

"Fine," I say, surprised he's not making me start this evening, but I'm not about to question his motives. I know better than to piss him off.

"Where's your fiancée?" Dante asks, and I'm quite confident he's not asking because he cares.

Unless you count him caring for his mafia family, but it's not out of any sense of kindness.

"Harper is on campus for the weekend," I say, leaving out the part where she's hanging out with her best friend Kensley.

"She's not spending the weekend with her son?" Dante seems disappointed.

"Her parents aren't speaking to her at the moment."

"How unfortunate," he says, but I don't see any remorse on his face for his involvement in this mess.

I lean against the wall, fold my arms across my chest and glare at him. "Right, coming from the man who insisted we tell her parents about our engagement over a dinner here," I seethe. I'm not the least bit happy about my father pulling all the strings.

It seems I have zero control over the situation, in part my own doing by trying to save Harper.

Would I do it all over again?

Absolutely.

"Speaking of the engagement. Your mother and I were talking, and we insist that you both have the wedding here, under our roof. We'll pay for everything. Your mother is happy to handle the wedding plans since you both are in school and Harper is, I'm sure, busy with her son."

"You're not serious." I stare at him like he just suggested decimating an entire population.

"I don't think February is too soon," Dante says. "We'll let you pick the date."

How fricking generous of him to let us choose our own wedding date. "Great," I grumble.

When the conversation is done, I head toward the library, finding Nova curled on the sofa reading under the lamplight.

"Have enough room for two?" I ask.

She holds up a finger, finishes her page and then slides a bookmark to keep her place. Nova keeps her voice low and quiet. "Have you heard anything about Rhys?"

"Your bodyguard? No, why?"

"I haven't seen him since my birthday party," Nova says. "He won't answer his phone when I call him. Don't you think that's weird?"

"Caden hasn't been around either," I point out. But we both know why he isn't under my father's roof anymore.

He was murdered.

"So, you do think something happened to Rhys!" Her eyes widen and then she covers her mouth, realizing that we have to talk quieter or take this conversation some place else if we don't want anyone to eavesdrop.

The last time we snuck into the hall closet, we got caught. At least out in the open, we're less suspicious, just two siblings hanging out together.

"I don't know, Nova. Maybe he has another assignment that's keeping him off the compound for a while. Did you ask your father about it?"

"Yeah, he told me to stop asking questions and then he assigned Nico as my personal security detail. Not that Nico does much. Since Mom and Dad gave me a car, I don't have to depend on one of their goons to drive me around town. Sometimes he comes with me, but he's not very friendly."

"Well, when you get to college, Nico won't be around," I say.

"Why do you think I pushed so hard for graduating early?" Nova smirks. "Rhys was awesome. He kept the fact I've been visiting you guys a secret. But he warned me that Dad's been asking questions and now that Nico is my new shadow for hire, he reports everything to my dad."

"Moreno knows that you were at our house Thursday and Friday?" I ask.

"Yes, I told Dad I wanted to watch the Narwhals game against the Wolverines and that it'd be late coming home, so I'd rather crash on your couch. I didn't have school on Friday, so he was fine with it since you were there."

"Any word on the little boy?" I ask, glancing in the direction of the basement.

"He's already been moved. Dad sent Mom and me out on an afternoon spending spree, which is so unlike him, unless he's up to no good. Did you see the news? They reported the kid dead, along with his family. Showed his photo for a good two minutes on the nightly news after the explosion leveled their home."

I curse and rub the back of my neck. "Any word on the investigation?"

It's obvious that my father was involved.

Nova stands and puts the book that she'd been reading back on the shelf. "Nothing, but we know the little boy is alive, Rylan Matthews."

"It's all so fucked up," I mutter, watching as Nova paces the length of the library.

"You have to stop him," Nova says, her gaze pleading with me to do something.

She's not the only one unhappy under this roof. I'm well aware that Harper is frustrated by my father, turns out Nova is as well, and so am I.

But I can't stop him. I can't go up against Dante when he has an army behind him.

"How do you think that's going to happen?" I tilt my head back on the sofa, staring up at the ceiling.

"He's making you work for him, *do something*."

Nova makes it sound so easy, like I could just put a gun to Dante's head, pull the trigger, and make all the horrible acts he's done vanish.

Life isn't that simple; neither is stopping the mafia boss.

The next morning after breakfast, I hear soft footsteps while I sip my coffee and glance up.

"What the hell are you doing here?" I ask, my gaze tightening on Ashton.

Dante closes the distance behind Ashton, apparently hearing my question. "I invited him," my father says.

"Why?" I put my coffee mug down, my appetite sated.

"Ashton is doing an internship for my organization," Dante says proudly. I imagine he's the son Dante always wanted, not me.

"Of course, he is," I mutter, glancing at Ashton, wondering how long they've been working together.

"He's going to help train you, get you up to speed on your shooting skills at the firing range this morning."

My shooting skills are zilch since I've never handled a gun, not after witnessing my father use one to commit murder.

"Can't we just train in the gym with weights or in hand-to-hand combat?" I'm one hell of a fighter. It helps that I play hockey; I'm used to getting roughed up and dishing it back out.

"No," Dante says. "You need to get over your fear and learn to fucking shoot a target."

He turns and decides that he's done as he walks away, leaving Ashton and me alone in the hallway.

"Scared to hold a gun?" Ashton is smirking at me, and I throw up my middle finger at him.

"Hardly, I've just never seen the need." I gesture to the compound around me. "I've got enough men doing my father's bidding. I don't need to be one of them."

Ashton steps closer and stares at me. "Turns out you do, since you work for him now."

I bite my tongue.

If Ashton is working for Dante, then anything I say or gripe about is bound to get repeated.

My best friend betrayed me, at least that's how it feels, and next time we're on the ice, I fully intend to return a little blood for blood.

We head to the shooting range and gear up.

I swallow the bile that rises in my throat.

Of course, my father would demand that I learn to shoot. He had tried during my teen years to invite me to the shooting range with him, but I always made up some excuse about school, homework, or hockey practice.

Dante is a smart man. He knew I wasn't interested, but he kept pushing.

Turns out, he wins.

I know the basics of how to hold a gun, using two hands, what the different parts of the gun are called. The thing is, though I've played shooter games on my console, I haven't picked up an actual gun, nor have I wanted to in the past decade.

Ashton gets me set up with a 9mm. He explains how it has a higher amount of muzzle energy, making it more effective at longer distances.

The weight of the gun is heavier than I imagined, and as I stare down the sight, there's no red dot or laser to guide my aim.

I already know my firing is going to be an embarrassment because I've never stepped foot in a shooting range.

But here I am.

It could be worse.

Dante could be teaching me.

Instead, I have Ashton, who shows me all the basics, which I already fucking know, thank you very much, and then he shoots and aims to kill.

He hits the target with a precision that makes my stomach roil.

Every shot hits the chest, dead center.

I turn off the safety, line up the sight with the target and shoot.

I hit the edge of the border of the paper, which at least is something. The gun has more of a recoil than I anticipated. Playing video games doesn't exactly get you prepared for the real thing.

"Again," Ashton commands, but I barely hear him over the headphones that I'm required to wear.

I keep shooting, my aim getting a little better but nowhere near as perfect as Ashton's, and it sucks.

I hate to admit I'm actually jealous of him.

───────

We spend a couple of hours at the shooting range, grab lunch, and then head back to the compound.

Since I'm the only one of us who owns a car, I drive.

"When did you start working for Dante?" I ask on our way back.

"A few weeks ago. Called me up after dinner and asked if I wanted to make a few bucks. Told me I'd get college credit too, which is more than I could have asked for."

Of course, he did.

"Are you going to be at the compound every weekend?" I ask. While I'm not thrilled that Ashton is working for my father, at least he's a buffer between Dante and me.

"Not sure," Ashton says.

"You don't know your hours?" I glance at him briefly.

"He gives me assignments, tells me when he needs my help with a job. It's not a big deal. Easy money and an even easier passing grade for my work-study that everyone's required to do."

"What kind of assignments?" I grumble, wondering if he has anything to do with Rhys missing or any involvement with the little boy, Rylan.

Ashton exhales a heavy breath. "That's above your pay grade."

"Are you fucking with me?"

Silence fills the vehicle, and Ashton reaches for the radio to turn it on.

I swat his hand away.

"Seriously, you're not going to tell me anything?" Annoyance pricks under my skin and I swerve the car off the road, slamming on the brakes. "Get the fuck out."

"What?" Ashton's eyes widen as I point at the car door.

"We're working together, and if you can't tell me what you're up to, then I can't trust you. Walk home."

Ashton's mouth is agape. "It's freezing outside, and we're twenty miles from your parents' place. There's nothing around here; we're in the middle of nowhere. You're not serious."

"I'm dead serious. Get out of my fucking car."

Ashton huffs and opens the door. "Your funeral." He steps out into the cold, the wind blasting me when he gets out. A moment later, he slams the door shut.

I hit the gas and pull back onto the road.

Not ten minutes later, my phone rings, repeatedly.

Nova's name flashes up on the dashboard as an incoming call.

After I ignore her the first two times, she keeps calling.

I finally answer.

"I'm busy right now," I say.

"You're fucking dead to me if you don't turn around and pick up Ashton," Nova shouts at me through the phone.

"Well, hello to you too."

"You're an asshole, do you know that?" Nova is on a roll.

"I'm just teaching him a lesson."

"Why?" Nova asks. "What'd he do that was so terrible that you decided to leave him on the side of a deserted road?"

My jaw tightens. "I don't owe you an explanation."

"Well, I already heard Ashton's side. If I have to drive over there and pick him up, you're dead to me."

I shift in my seat, glancing in the rearview. I haven't seen a car driving in the opposite direction since dropping Ashton on the side of the road. "I would have thought you'd be taking my side, since we're family," I say.

"Yeah, well, you're becoming more like your father every day."

I hang up on Nova, but she calls right back.

"See!" she shouts at me. "You're proving my point. Quit being a stubborn jackass and go get Ashton."

"Fine!" I shout and do a U-turn on the two-lane road. "I don't know why you care about Ashton. You always complain that he watches shitty documentaries and hogs all the popcorn."

I'm met with her silence.

Finally stumped her.

About damn time!

"Just pick him up."

I grumble at her. "I am, I've already turned around. I'll be there in a few minutes."

This time I hang up for good, and a minute later, I can see Ashton walking in the distance, heading in my direction.

I contemplate driving past him, just to be an asshole, but think better of it. I've seen a few lone snowflakes already; the weather could be turning any minute.

I pull to a stop, unlock the car door and he silently gets in.

"You called my sister to tattle on me. Real mafia of you," I say, turning the car back around in the direction I was previously heading.

Ashton secures his seatbelt while I hit the gas, trying to make up for time. Snow slowly begins to blanket the sky, but it hasn't laid yet on the ground.

"Would you have rather I called your father?"

Point taken.

I reach for the radio and let the music drown out the silence, but it does nothing to dispel the tension in the car as we head back to the compound.

We leave early Sunday morning, and as a peace offering, I drive Ashton with me back to campus.

The tension is still heavy between us, but we had spent most of Saturday evening pretending everything was fine.

It seems neither of us wanted to piss off Dante, who was in a vile mood.

"You don't have to worry about me replacing you," Ashton says as we near the exit.

"What are you talking about?"

"This internship for Ricci Enterprises, it's just for the semester."

I snort. Is that what he really thinks will happen? My father will just let him work for a couple of months for the family business and then leave.

He's stupider than I thought.

"You're an idiot," I mutter as I turn onto the main road that leads us near campus.

"I fully intend to work for *my* father after I graduate. Dante is just a means to an end."

He's got to be joking. "Does he know that, because Dante doesn't just let men walk away after everything they've been involved in and seen?"

"Aurelio and Dante are old friends. I'm not worried."

I pull up out front of our building.

"You should be."

"Why are you so worried about me? Worry about your girlfriend and her kid."

I pull into a parking spot, my breathing catching in my throat. "Is that a threat?"

I kill the engine, and Ashton unbuckles, hopping out of the car before answering me.

I climb out of the car, appalled that he hasn't even answered me yet.

"If you come after Harper or Zeke, I will kill you."

Ashton grabs his bag from the trunk and holds up his hands. "Relax, I'm not going to go anywhere near your girlfriend."

"Or her son," I grit between clenched teeth.

I reach for my bag, grabbing it and slamming the trunk shut.

"I'm not in the business of hurting little kids, and neither is your father. Just don't fuck this up and everything will be fine."

"Another threat. You sound more like Dante every second you're in that house," I shoot back.

"Thanks," Ashton flashes a smile my way. "Your dad would be so proud." He heads up the walkway toward the front door.

Bastard.

I lunge at Ashton before he makes it inside, yanking him back around to face me as my fist lands blow after blow to his face.

The sting feels good across my knuckles.

His arm comes up, blocking another repeated blow and uppercuts me across my jaw.

I stumble backward for a second.

Fuck, that hurts.

Liam comes running outside, apparently hearing the commotion.

He grabs me from behind, yanking me off Ashton, breaking up the fight.

It's not the first fight he's had to break up, but it's never been off the ice.

"What the hell is wrong with the two of you?" Liam shouts at us. He shoves us inside like a den mother disappointed in her young.

"He started it!" Ashton points at me.

"Yeah, well, he threatened my fiancée and her son," I growl, ready for another round if Liam releases his hold on me.

NINE

When Luca shows up to class, I can't stop staring at him.

But it's not in the typical way, where he catches my eye and my body heats up.

Okay, maybe it is, but it's a different heat, the kind that burns with anger and concern, not lust.

"What the hell happened in practice?" I ask.

Luca is sporting a bruised chin and a split lip.

"Wasn't practice."

That's the only answer I get because the professor begins his lecture and Luca pretends to pay attention in economics class.

That's a first for him. He has a notebook out, and his hand is moving along the page.

Is he actually taking notes?

One glance at the paper, and I see he's doodling, like his mind is wandering and he's not even aware of what he's drawing.

Or maybe he is aware, but it's nothing specific. His pencil keeps gliding across the page, and I know he feels me staring at him because his shoulders tense.

Instead of him saying anything, he ignores me.

"Put your notebooks, laptops, everything away except a pen or pencil. We're having a pop quiz," the professor announces in the last twenty minutes of lecture.

Fuck me.

I didn't get to study with Luca over the weekend. I had hoped that we'd get together Sunday evening, after he came home from his father's and after hockey practice.

But when I texted him, he had told me he was too tired to hang out or study.

And with the dark circles under his eyes and the bruise on his cheek, I'm filled with worry.

If he didn't get the bruises from practice, did it happen when he was at his parents' house?

Was it the mafia that did this to him?

The teaching assistant for the class hands out our quizzes, row by row. I hand one to Luca, staring at him, wanting to ask about the mafia, his father, but I can't, not here, not in class.

His eyes meet mine, and he forces a smile.

But I don't smile back.

I can't.

All I'm filled with is worry.

Concern for him.

Fear for my son.

I don't even care what happens to me; it's Zeke who's my priority.

Would it be safer to disappear with Zeke? I know Luca was against it, because he believed his father could find us anywhere, but that can't be true.

I'll ask him about it after class, because I worry that whatever happened to Luca, like the split lip and bruised cheek, will happen to my son.

Maybe not today, when he's two, but when he gets older.

"All eyes on your quiz. This isn't a group effort," the professor scolds, and I glance from Luca down to the paper in front of me.

I'm not confident in the answers that I put down; some of them are multiple choice, and even those options seem like two answers might fit. The essay portion, I'm probably screwed.

I glance up to hand in my assignment because we've been instructed that once we're done, we can leave.

Luca has already finished. I didn't notice him get up and walk down the aisle to turn in his quiz.

I drop mine off on the professor's desk and sling my backpack over my shoulder, heading out of the lecture hall.

Luca leans against the wall, his arms folded across his chest.

"You waited for me," I whisper, surprised he didn't bolt out after, like I thought he had done.

"When don't I walk you to your next class?" Luca asks, and he accompanies me outside.

I button my coat as we walk; the cold air whipping around us.

"Are you going to tell me how you got—" I gesture at my face, wanting to know about his bruises.

"Ashton."

"What? How did that happen?"

Luca's gaze is on the sidewalk, his head down, his eyes refusing to meet mine. "I don't want to talk about it."

"Ashton assaulted you. How can you not want to talk about it?"

He glances at me for a brief second and then his attention is back on the cement. "I threw the first punch."

Fuck.

That was *not* what I was expecting to hear from him. "Okay," I say slowly and shuffle my backpack from one shoulder to the other.

"Here, give me that," Luca offers, taking my backpack with my books and laptop, carrying it for me across campus.

"Thanks."

"I thought about skipping class today," Luca says and then glances at me, "but I wanted to talk to you."

"About the fight?" Not that he's really explained any of it to me.

I still don't know what Ashton and Luca were fighting about. Maybe I can ask Ashton if he shows up during lunch again. He has been making it a habit lately.

Is it because he has a thing for Kensley?

"Not about the fight. About something Dante said to me over the weekend."

"Oh." I exhale forcefully, and my breath hovers in the air.

"The wedding," Luca says, and I stop walking.

The building is up ahead, and we have time since we finished the quiz early. "What'd your father say about our wedding?" My stomach is turbulent at the mention of our wedding, but I need to know what brought Luca all the way to class after clearly avoiding me last night.

"He wants us to marry in February."

"This February?" My voice raises an octave. I hadn't quite intended to sound so squeaky, but he caught me off guard with that comment.

"With school and your son, he's willing to have Nikki plan the wedding for us and have it at their home."

"Of course, he is. Where he has complete control of everything," I mutter. "What'd you tell him?"

Luca stalls, staring at me. "Not really much. He's intimidating as fuck!"

I huff and take a step back. "I know, he's about to be my father-in-law." That thought turns my stomach even more sour, like I just had bad milk.

"The bright side was he told me we could choose the date."

Seriously?

"How generous of him," I mock and turn on my heels, walking to my next class.

"You're mad," Luca says. It's not a question, but clearly an observation, because I'm steaming right now.

"I'm not happy!" I shout, and Luca strides right alongside me. Even as I pick up pace, with ease, he's at my side.

"Are you mad at me—or Dante?" Luca asks.

His question is fair.

Luca is a part of this as much as I am, if not more so because he was doing the good deed in trying to save my life. I'll never be able to repay him for that, but maybe I can offer him a way out.

"I'm—frustrated!" I glare at him. "I know this isn't your fault. I blame your father, but I still, I wish you could just tell him to go fuck off and leave us alone."

"He's mafia, babe," Luca says with a faint smile. "If I could say that to him, then I'd be running the empire."

No one talks back to Dante Ricci.

I slow my pace as we approach the Fitzroy building for my next class. He hands over my backpack, carefully putting it over my shoulder, his hands gentle yet firm.

"I don't want to fight with you," Luca says.

I nod slowly. "I know. None of this is what *we* want." I step closer, stand on my tiptoes and press a soft kiss to his cheek. "Tell your mom I'll do whatever she wants for the wedding. I'll meet up with her if she wants to go dress shopping, just, whatever. Let's not get on your family's bad side."

Luca's eyes tighten. "Are you sure?"

"Don't ask me again, because my answer might not be yes."

———

Kensley and I head to the arena, excitement bubbling within me at seeing Luca play tonight.

"I feel like we don't hang out enough," Kensley admits on our walk to the arena.

"I'm sorry," I immediately apologize, knowing that it's my fault entirely. I've been spending more time with Luca, and I know with the wedding planning on the horizon, we'll be spending even less time together.

Not to mention after Zeke comes to live with us.

Everything is going to change.

"No, don't apologize. I just feel like I'm missing some very big pieces to the puzzle." Kensley stops walking and stares at me.

It's just the two of us, but I glance around, making sure no one is nearby watching us or eavesdropping.

I've gotten into the habit of double-checking my surroundings constantly.

"See! You seem so paranoid lately. Do you have a stalker?" Kensley asks.

I laugh, and I see relief flood her features. "No."

"What's going on? I get why you didn't mention Zeke when we first met. We were just becoming friends, he wasn't on campus. You probably wanted a normal college experience or whatever—" Kensley says and waves her hand. "But the engagement to Luca, I've been holding my tongue, but I can't just keep quiet anymore."

"You don't approve?" I ask, expecting her to say yes.

"I think you're hiding something. I mean, you were denying you even had feelings for him at the beginning of the semester, and then next thing I know, you two are engaged, but there's no ring. Which doesn't necessarily mean anything, and no judgment if you love him, but I don't know. Something feels off."

Kensley is more than just a little suspicious, and I can't blame her.

"You can trust me," Kensley says. "I promise, whatever you say will be kept in confidence."

I exhale sharply and glance around once more.

There are a few people coming in our direction and I pull her off the sidewalk, waiting until they pass.

"You can't tell anyone, not Luca, and not even Ashton."

Kensley smirks. "Do you think I see Ashton without you? I promise I won't say anything, now spill it, girl."

"Luca is marrying me to protect me," I whisper. "His family is mafia, and I wandered into something I shouldn't have." I leave out the specifics because I don't want Kensley to know more than she already does.

Telling her puts her life in danger, which is selfish of me, but I need her help.

"His father ordered my death."

"Holy shit. Are you serious?" Kensley gasps and then covers her mouth with her hand.

"Luca proposed a different solution, that we marry, which makes me part of their family. He saves my life, and in return, I'm his wife."

"What does he get out of it?" Kensley asks and then looks me over. "Never mind."

"What's that supposed to mean?" I chock.

"Oh, come on, you're cute. He's had his eyes on you for how long? You can't be oblivious to his crush. Now, he gets you."

"Forever," I remind her.

"There's always divorce—unless they kill their ex-wives?"

I don't recall any mention of divorce or previous marriages among his family members. "Listen, you can't tell anyone. You promised."

"You have my word. It'll go with me to the grave."

"Good, because I'm going to need your help."

We finish our private chat before we head the rest of the way to the arena. We're not as early as we had intended. My fault, but I'm glad that I finally have someone else to confide in.

We grab our seats, and the Narwhals are already on the ice warming up.

I'm buried in the crowd, and while I'm not sure Luca sees me, I did text him that I'd be at his game tonight.

Turns out, I might actually be enjoying hockey. Not that I have the slightest clue what's happening, but watching Luca play and seeing him win has been a highlight of my week.

He's been hot on the ice and he doesn't disappoint, scoring two of the four goals tonight.

He does end up in the penalty box twice, but neither fight he started. Which at least I feel better about, considering what happened between him and Ashton a couple of days ago.

The bruise isn't nearly as noticeable on his face, and his split lip has already healed.

Unlike last time when we waited by our seats, this time, we wait outside the team's locker room, at his insistence.

Kensley keeps me company, and since they had a big win, I imagine they'll want to celebrate and blow off some steam at their afterparty at the house.

The door swings open, and Chase and Liam exit the locker room.

I recognize both of them from the party, and though I know Liam lives with Luca, I hardly ever see him around the house. He's always out, doing whatever it is that he does.

The couple of times I've seen him, he's dropping in, grabbing something from his room and then jetting out.

"Hey, Liam," I say, giving a nod.

Next semester, he's going to be one of our

housemates, though if it's anything like this semester has been, he'll barely be around.

Luca never mentioned Liam having a girlfriend, but he must if he's always sleeping elsewhere every night.

Right?

"You're Luca's fiancée," Chase says, walking over toward me.

Apparently, the guy's heard the news. It was bound to get out eventually, especially with the living arrangements for next semester.

"That's right," I say, standing straighter, trying not to feel intimidated by two very good-looking hockey players who are several inches taller than I am.

"Did he knock you up?" Chase asks, glancing me over from head to toe, but his eyes linger a few moments on my stomach.

The locker room door swings open, and Luca steps out, showered and dressed.

Luca is glowing, absolutely radiant after tonight's game, but that quickly turns to a fiery heat as he glares at Chase and then Liam.

"Are they giving you a hard time?" Luca scowls and hurries over to sling an arm around my shoulder.

I keep forgetting whether this is the real Luca or him pretending to be in love with me. The lines seem really blurry as of late.

"They're just asking about our engagement," I say, forcing a smile, trying to ease the tension.

I still don't know what ticked Luca off to get into a fight with Ashton. The last thing I want is for Luca to go head-on brawling with his other teammates. Not only is it terrible for team morale, but I don't want anything to happen to Luca.

He doesn't need to fight for me.

"They're just jealous." Luca snarls at them and then spins around, his mouth capturing mine, closing the distance in haste, kissing me.

His leg slides between my thighs, nudging them apart as he pins me against the wall, and for a moment, I wonder how far he wants this to go between us, with his teammates watching.

It definitely feels like it's for show.

I lean into the kiss, parting my lips, letting him take the lead but hungrily desiring him. Need quickly takes hold, my fingers clawing at his shirt, his back, as he lifts me against him and I wrap my legs around him.

I could gladly fuck him if it would shut them all up.

We part for a brief second, catching air, our foreheads leaning against one another. Then again, I have quite a bit of doubt if this is all an act, because he's convinced even me.

I can feel his desire poking me, and my own insides are throbbing for more.

"Get a room," Liam groans and smacks his buddy Chase on the shoulder. "Let's go back to my place, celebrate the win."

"I think I'm just going to call it a night," Kensley says.

I untangle from Luca's embrace, my legs wobbly as he holds me steady against the wall, his hands firmly planted on my hips.

"Are you sure?" I ask. "We should hang out more."

Kensley smiles and stares at Luca. "Please don't take

this the wrong way, but I don't want to watch the two of you make out all night or fuck on the couch."

"We didn't—" I frown, not understanding her judgment. We were very careful to go upstairs at the last party and keep everything private, between just the two of us.

"It's okay, I don't mind dropping you off at home," Luca offers.

After we drop Kensley off at her dorm, Luca and I drive back to his place. I appreciate the stillness and that it's just the two of us for a few brief moments of peace and quiet before we step foot into his place.

I know the team is celebrating and I'm happy for them; they deserve the win and Luca is the reason for it, but I still miss just the little quiet moments between the two of us.

"What are you doing for Thanksgiving?" Luca asks as he pulls up to his building. "It's right around the corner."

He's clearly coming off the adrenaline high as he drives me back to his place for the afterparty. I feel his energy sizzling, and I reach for his hand, wanting to be his rock. "Can I just stay in the dorms and hide from the world?"

"What about Zeke?"

A heavy sigh finds my lips. "I don't think my parents are going to be happy with me when I show up for Thanksgiving. I know they're going to try to talk me out of marrying you, moving in together next semester, all of it."

He nods slowly and parks the car but leaves it running. I unbuckle, ready to get out, but he hasn't shut off the engine.

The conversation clearly isn't over for him.

He unbuckles his seatbelt and turns to face me.

"I could come with you," he says.

I open my mouth, considering his suggestion, and then shut it.

"What's that look?" Luca asks, staring at me curiously. He reaches out, his hand grazing my cheek.

"What about your family and your parents? Do you

think Dante is going to be okay with you missing Thanksgiving?"

Luca shrugs and glances at the house. "I missed it last year. Didn't kill him."

"Too bad," I quip and wince. "Sorry."

"Don't ever apologize for being honest with me. That's all I'd ever ask of you," Luca says.

I know he's right. I haven't always been honest with him. I hid Zeke from him, but at the time, we weren't dating and there hadn't been a good time to reveal that I had a son. I have no intention of hiding anything from him ever again.

"So, Thanksgiving at my parents' house?" Just saying it aloud brings nausea to my lips.

"If we're both invited," Luca says. "I go where you go."

Reaching for his hand, I take it in mine. "You don't have to suffer with me, because it will be impossible to get through the meal without fighting."

Luca reaches for me, pulling me closer. "I'm not going to let you go through that alone. We're in this together. Please don't ever forget that."

———

I dread when the fourth Thursday of November rolls around.

Thanksgiving.

Luca agreed to come with me, so we could commiserate in hell together.

While my parents aren't mafia, they're also not the least bit quiet about their opinions. Growing up, I never thought it could be a bad trait until I got pregnant at fifteen.

Then the parents all my friends loved, who saw them as their own mom and dad, had felt as though they'd turned on me.

They wanted me to take care of my little problem, so it wouldn't affect my future.

My body, my choice, I had told them.

I hadn't wanted to go through with the pregnancy, but I'd been rebelling, and whatever they wanted, I did the opposite.

Maybe they'd known all along, and it had been some reverse psychology crap they pulled on me.

Turns out, pregnancy was a bitch that I didn't see coming, and raising a baby, that was even harder.

But they supported whatever decision I made.

I still believe I made the right decision, even though it's been difficult for everyone. Zeke is amazing. I just wish I spent more time with him, and it seems my wish is being granted.

Whether I'm ready for it or not.

Food is on the table, my grandmother's china, and real silverware beside our plates. It's the only time we're allowed to use the special dishes; otherwise, they're kept neatly tucked away on the top shelf, out of reach.

Zeke gets a plastic plate, which is wise considering he likes to drop his plate on the floor. Most of the time, I just feed him in the highchair when I'm with him, or in the case of at someone's home who has a carpeted dining room, then I hand feed him, which he detests.

"Thank you for including me tonight," Luca says, smiling as he tries to break the tension.

We've barely been here for twenty minutes, the food already prepared. We probably should have arrived earlier, but I honestly didn't want to.

I was trembling and crying, having a panic attack. Luca managed to calm me down, in strangely much the same manner as his mother had done the first time we'd gone to lunch together.

"Well, it was our daughter who invited you." Dad glares at Luca.

"Dad, I wanted you to get to know Luca." I reach for Luca's hand, giving it a squeeze. "He's important to me. I would hope that you'd take the time to get to know someone who means that much to me."

"I know all I need to," Dad says. "He's interested in only one thing with my daughter!"

Catrina clears her throat and glares at her husband. "Oh, settle down, Jack. Like we weren't madly in love when we first met."

"We didn't get hitched after a month."

Catrina forces a smile. "No, we most certainly did not. But perhaps we should give the benefit of the doubt to these two lovebirds and let them explain to us why they wish to rush into marriage and family life."

My dad watches Mom carefully before saying, "Luca, why don't you start? Since you'll instantly become a father to Zeke when you marry my daughter."

———

Three weeks later, when Luca is forced to help Dante with whatever mafia business they're up to, Nikki, Paige, Nova, and I go dress shopping for a wedding gown.

Of course, it's not just the girls.

Like last time, Moreno is babysitting us.

"Can we really get a dress by February?" I ask.

It's already December, and I keep hoping Nikki will come to her senses, talk her husband into pushing back the wedding, at least until we graduate.

That's part of the reason I agreed to go dress shopping with his mom. But I didn't expect Nikki to invite Nova's mother along. At least Paige had the sense to suggest Nova join us too.

Nova hangs out with me in the dressing room while Paige and Nikki keep procuring dresses for me to try on.

"We can have a dress by the end of January if we order it from this shop," Nikki says. "Of course, it'll need alterations, but we have a seamstress who can make those adjustments within a few weeks. Which puts us at the end of February..." Her voice trails off.

"That's fine. I was thinking the last Saturday in February." Personally, I was thinking February twenty-ninth since it's not a leap year, but I refrain from being a smartass.

Nikki is being pleasant, as is Paige, and I don't want Dante getting wind that I'm causing trouble.

The last thing I want is to hurt Luca.

"I really like the first dress," Nova says to me as I try on the fourth or fifth for the afternoon.

I've already lost count.

"No, the mermaid style doesn't do my body any favors." I don't have the breasts to wear the dress, or the curves. I look like a lumpy tree.

"I agree with Harper," Paige says. "We'll find something better, something that suits you." She shoves another dress at me to try on, pushing through the cloth barrier of a door.

Nova grabs the gown and helps me into the dress while the parents are outside perusing the store for available dresses to try on. She leans in close, whispering so that no one else can hear, "Are you really going to go through with marrying Luca?"

"Do I have a choice?" I ask, glancing over my shoulder at her.

I want to trust Nova, but her family can't be trusted, which puts her in my uncertainty category.

I trust Luca, and his family can't be trusted.

"You could tell them no," Nova whispers.

I glance at her skeptically. "Do you think that will work with Dante?"

Nova shrugs and sits on the bench in the dressing room. "Probably not. I just hate seeing you two get married under these pretenses. It's just not what either of you want."

"Have you spoken with Luca?" I ask, wondering what he's been saying to Nova about the upcoming wedding.

Luca and I haven't done a single lick of wedding planning ourselves. We hadn't specifically set a date yet either until today, when I just announced it to Nikki.

The two of us had talked about it privately, but we had been hoping the longer we waited, maybe we could push the wedding back a tiny bit longer.

"He avoids wedding discussions, but I kind of figured that was all guys. I mean, I know the reason you two are getting hitched—" She stares at me seriously. "Dante is forcing you. But there has to be another way."

"There isn't," I whisper, "and we shouldn't talk about this around your mother or Luca's because whatever gets overheard will come back to bite us in the ass."

"Well, at least Dad's waiting outside," Nova says.

Moreno drove us and insisted he come into the store, but the shop is already quite small and crowded between the dresses and the four of us, plus the two ladies working the shop. Paige told him to grab a coffee and give the girls some time alone.

He grumbled but hasn't stepped foot back into the boutique. He's outside, probably glaring at anyone who so much as thinks about coming inside the bridal shop.

Nova helps secure the back of the gown, which is much too big, but she cinches it with clips to get a feel for how it should fit. "What do you think about this dress?"

I pull open the purple velvet curtain and step out, standing in front of the full-length mirror. The dress is absolutely stunning, with long lace sleeves and an A-line frame that fans out at just the right place.

"This is the one," I say, certain that if I were ever to get married, this would be the dress.

I chew on my bottom lip, my fingers grazing over the downy material. I didn't even glance at the price tag.

"How soon can we get this one in her size?" Nikki asks the store clerk.

She comes up, glancing at the tag tucked into the back of the gown, and jots the information down before returning. "We have two of those in stock in our warehouse in her size. It usually takes a couple of weeks, but we can put in a special request to have it delivered by Friday for a pick-up in store. Would that be okay?"

The way the girl who runs the shop looks at Nikki, I feel the hair on my arms tingle.

"Yes, we'll come by Saturday next week to try it on and pick it up," Nikki says, already deciding my schedule for me.

Next week is Christmas.

Nova holds the train of the gown while I saunter back into the dressing room and disrobe. She grabs the curtain, closing it for me before un-cinching the clips at the back, helping me out of the elegant gown.

"That's definitely the one," Nova says, smiling as I put my clothes back on.

"Will you be wearing a veil?" the store clerk asks while I put my coat on and then yank the curtain open.

"I hadn't really thought about it," I say.

"Yes, we're going traditional," Nikki says and then wraps an arm around my shoulders. "If you don't like it, you don't have to wear it, but we should at least have it for the wedding. Especially for pictures."

"Right."

So much for not having to wear it, if I'm being forced to have it on for photographs.

"Thanks, Mom," I say, the words slightly forced, but I offer a smile, trying to show my appreciation.

If I can get on anyone's good side, it's definitely Nikki, and I'm going to need her in my corner.

Nikki's smile brightens when she hears me call her *Mom*. She wraps an arm around my shoulders. "I'm so excited to have you as part of our family, Harper."

TEN

NOVA

I hurry down the stairs Christmas Day, excited that Ashton will be joining us for the holiday.

"What's got you up so early?" Luca asks, sipping a mug of piping hot coffee.

"You're here already!" Excitement overwhelms me as I rush over to give my brother a hug. "Merry Christmas! Did you come by yourself?"

I'm glancing around, hoping Ashton is somewhere in this house, but trying my best to be inconspicuous.

Discreet isn't my middle name.

"Just me and Ashton right now. He's helping Dante by moving some furniture around upstairs. I'm going to swing by Harper's parents' and pick her and Zeke up in about an hour."

"They're not all coming over?" I ask. I know Mom and Dad invited them, along with Luca's parents, but after what I heard happened the last time they visited, I guess I shouldn't be all that surprised.

Luca frowns. "I'm not even sure they'll be at the wedding."

"Don't worry," I say and grab myself a cup of coffee but pour tons of flavored creamer into it to kill the bitterness. "I'm sure they'll come around. It's their grandson they'll miss out on if they don't."

"Yeah," Luca says and sips from the mug. "I hope you're right."

He leans against the kitchen counter, watching me prepare my coffee.

"How's the packing going?" Luca asks.

Next week, we move into the new house that we're renting. "Good. I'm mostly done. I heard Dad on the phone, trying to convince the current tenants to move out by Christmas."

Luca laughs. "I can only imagine how well that's going."

"He was cursing and storming into Dante's office, still on the phone." I shrug. "I didn't get to hear the rest."

He takes another sip from the mug. "Doesn't matter. What's the difference in one more week? Less than, since we move in on the first of the month."

"Twenty-eighth," Dad says, coming up from behind.

The man is pure stealth when he wants to be. "We managed to get you a few extra days before classes resume. You move on the twenty-eighth of December."

"You really wanted me out this year." I glare at Dad, but I'm not angry with him. He and Dante were trying to be helpful. They're always looking after family, putting us first.

"Dante and I wanted to make sure there was ample time to get everyone settled before your first day.

Especially with Zeke, for whom we've handled all the nursery arrangements."

"What?" Luca turns and faces my father, Moreno.

"It was supposed to be a surprise for Harper, but your father and I ordered a toddler bed and some things for Zeke."

I can't read Luca's features. He's masking his emotions right now.

"I'm sure Harper and Luca appreciate your help," I offer, trying to smooth things over. That was nice of Dante and Dad.

"Don't put words in my mouth," Luca snaps at me.

I step out of the kitchen, giving Luca his space and leaving him to deal with my father.

"What's wrong, son?"

While Dad isn't Luca's biological father, he's helped raise him as much as Dante has.

"I just wish you'd told me. We've been trying to scrape up money to make sure Zeke is cared for when we have him. I've been looking at taking on a part-time job, so has Harper."

I stand in the hallway, eavesdropping, careful not to be seen. But I'm curious, because Luca never mentioned he was looking for work. I can't imagine he even has time to work, with school and hockey getting in the way.

"Dante isn't going to want that for you. You work for him. You'll be spread too thin. And I've talked to him; he's agreed to pay you the same as Ashton."

"Wonderful," Luca says, but there's no hint of happiness in his tone.

"Listen, if you really don't love Harper, there's another way out of this—"

He scoffs, and I can hear the mug clattering and breaking, possibly in the sink. I glance over the corner to see if he threw it, but there are no shattered pieces on the floor.

Definitely the sink.

"I'm not harming a hair on her head or her son's," Luca says. "And if you so much as suggest it—"

"I wouldn't," Dad says. "I'm just trying to look out for you, Luca. I've always seen you as my own."

Footsteps patter over the marble flooring, and they're definitely coming from the staircase.

Eavesdropping is over. I hurry down the hall so as not to be caught when I glance up and notice Ashton and Dante approaching.

"Hey." My eyes light up, and I try my damndest not to seem too eager to see Ashton. "Merry Christmas."

Dante wanders past us, not even paying me the least bit of attention. I'm just an annoyance to him, probably the same as Luca.

Except Luca is his son.

Ashton waits a beat before the smile stretches across his face, and he pulls me into a hug. "Merry Christmas, Nova." He plants his lips on mine, and instantly, I freeze.

I push him away, eyes wide in horror.

"What are you doing?" I ask, but I'm mostly thinking *anyone can see us!*

Ashton points up at the mistletoe in the hallway. "I put that up this morning."

I jab him in the elbow and reach for his hand, dragging him away from prying eyes or the surveillance cameras. I know every secretive spot that can't be seen.

"Come with me." I usher him into the hall closet with me. The stained-glass window filters the daylight just enough to keep our presence hidden.

I saunter to the back of the closet, pulling him with me. "I've been wanting to kiss you," I whisper, tiptoeing to reach his lips.

Ashton is several inches taller than I am, and he leans down, scooping me into his arms and sitting on the bench, tugging me onto his lap.

Our mouths fuse with a fiery heat that builds like a volcano, waiting to erupt.

His fingers trail across my hip and then up to my neck. He gently guides the edge of my turtleneck down, taking witness of his mark having mostly disappeared.

"Did anyone ask about it?"

"The giant hickey you gave me?" I laugh and pull

back slightly. "Thankfully, I have plenty of sweaters with high enough collars, no one thought to ask."

Ashton doesn't apologize.

He grins.

"I kind of wish you would show everyone. Let them know you're mine," Ashton says, and then he steals another taste from my lips.

His hands are back around my hips, keeping me pressed against him on his lap.

"Possessive much?" I mumble, quite pleased with his attachment to me.

From what I've heard and seen, he doesn't sleep with anyone twice. The mere fact he's still interested has me mentally doing somersaults.

He's staring at my lips, like they're the main focus of his world. "Don't label me," Ashton says and plants a quick kiss on my mouth.

I whimper from the loss of contact and run my fingers through his hair. I pull his gaze up to meet mine. "Do you really want my brother finding out about us?" I ask.

He huffs, and the kisses are momentarily stopped once again. "No, but the entire team knows. We weren't exactly being quiet. Everyone saw us at the party after the game that night."

Actually, we were being quiet, but it was us making out and everyone watching that has rumors flying around us.

"How long until Luca finds out?" I ask. I can't help but wonder if I should tell him, or if Ashton should do it. They're teammates and best friends.

But I'm his sister.

"Pretty soon if he comes looking for us," Ashton says, and I grumble, standing up. Already, I miss the warm feel of his hands on my body.

He stands and brushes a stray hair behind my ear. "You look flushed. Go to the bathroom and cool off for a few minutes."

"And what about you?" I ask.

"What about me?" His smile vanishes. "I'm cool as a cucumber."

I glance down his body and eye his jeans, where his cock is hidden away. "Really?"

"I'll wait it out in here for a few," Ashton says and drops one more kiss on my lips before I sneak out of the hall closet and hope no one notices me.

———

I'm more than just a tad excited when the twenty-eighth rolls around and we move into the rental house on campus.

It's a nicer property than the dorms that I toured, and I still can't believe it's ours for the semester.

The house is a five-bedroom two-story, with lots of living room and study space. It's bigger than Luca's previous digs, which housed him, Ashton, Liam, and Jessie.

Funny enough, I never met Jessie. Not when I visited Luca's house on weekends or even when we moved out. He was never around, even less than Liam, who barely shows his face at home.

Which is fine with me. Living with boys isn't my first choice, but Dad insisted I stay in the same house as Harper and Luca. I find the whole situation a bit strange since they'll be married soon and Harper has a kid, but whatever.

As long as Zeke isn't crying in the middle of the night or keeping me from studying.

I haven't really spent much time with the little one. I met him on Christmas Day and gave him lots of tickles and cuddles.

He was enthralled with the toy train set that Dante and Nikki got him, which seemed to keep him pretty entertained, except when Harper had to chase after him, repeatedly.

Harper and Luca are down the hallway, with Zeke directly next door.

Ashton's room is at the opposite end of the hallway. "I call dibs on this room!" I say, grabbing the one across from Ashton, before I even so much as open the door to ascertain its size.

Ashton's door is wide open, and he lies on his bed, reading a magazine.

I poke my head in, curious if he's just taking a break or finished already.

There aren't any boxes in his room, nothing for him to unpack. He could help in the kitchen, but he's hiding out, probably until someone else notices.

"All done in here?" I ask.

He points at the dresser. "I just had them move it with my clothes inside." The smug look on his face greets me.

"You want to help me?"

"I'll pass," Ashton says and flips the page of his magazine.

"Okay, I wasn't asking."

He grumbles and shuts the magazine, climbing off the mattress. He stalks across the hallway, glances down in the direction of Luca and Harper's room before hurrying into my room and shutting the door rather abruptly.

"I said help." I laugh, glaring up at him as I open a packed box and inspect the contents.

"Oh, I have a few ideas for helping." He wiggles his eyebrows at me. "Not sure they involve cardboard, though." Ashton gestures at the boxes at my feet.

"You're useless," I grumble and dump all my clothes on the bed, on top of him.

Ashton laughs and grabs a pair of my yellow bikini panties and twirls them on his finger. "Look what I can do."

"You can put my stuff in that top drawer," I say and point at the dresser.

He mumbles something under his breath.

"What's that?" I glare at him.

"Feels like we're married. You, bossing me around."

"Well, we are living together." I smirk and put my hands on my hips. "Better get used to it, boyfriend."

Ashton rolls his eyes and throws a pair of my panties at me.

I catch them as they land on my chest.

Ashton wrestles out of the clothes and stands, leaving all my things on my mattress. "This is boring. I'm going to see if—"

"If what—Harper and Luca need help? You'll help them unpack?" I glare at him. "There are dishes and pots and pans that still need unpacking in the kitchen," I remind him.

He's less than useless. I'm happy that his room is done, but he's been zero help with the rest of the house.

"I was going to see if they need help with Zeke," Ashton says as he hurries to the door.

I almost feel bad, remembering that my brother and his girlfriend have a kid. Right. Zeke.

"Okay, fine. But don't teach that kid anything bad," I warn him. "No fart noises or anything stupid."

"First up on the agenda, fart noises it is," Ashton teases, and I yank my pillow off the mattress and fling it at him.

He ducks, and the pillow hits my door. He bends down, picks it up and tosses it back on the bed.

"I'll take a raincheck for the pillow fight," Ashton says and tosses open my bedroom door. He hurries out into the hallway. Apparently, he couldn't get out fast enough.

"And spoiling Zeke is my job!" I shout. "Don't forget that. I'm his aunt!"

Ten minutes later, Zeke comes tearing into my room screaming in hysterics.

I glance up and Ashton is chasing after him, his arms out like a monster. "I'm going to get you," Ashton roars in a deep voice, and Zeke rushes at me, throwing his arms around my leg.

"You're scaring him!" I bend down, lifting Zeke into my arms.

There are no tears as I examine him a little more closely, just smiles and laughter. He holds out his arms to Ashton.

"The kid loves me," Ashton beams and takes him from my arms. "I'm his favorite."

"Good, because I'm still mad that you're not helping." I pretend to glare at him, but it's hard to stay mad when I see how good he is with Zeke. And I hate to admit that he is helping, just in a different manner.

"Zeke, do you want to help this pretty girl put her panties away?" Ashton asks Zeke.

My eyes widen in horror. "Oh my gosh. I swear you're going to corrupt him! Harper!" I squeal.

"Is Zeke bothering you?" Harper's voice carries from down the hallway.

This time, Ashton glares at me. "Everything's fine! Nova is being a drama queen."

I want to throw something at him, but he's holding Zeke in his arms.

"You're such a—" I can't even curse because the kid is staring right at me!

"Such a what?" Ashton grins, clearly amused by the situation as he keeps Zeke close to his chest. He turns Zeke to face me, and then Ashton sticks his tongue out at me and uses Zeke as a human shield.

"I can't with you!" I point at the door. "Out! No boys allowed!"

"Somebody's in a mood." Ashton laughs, clearly amused by my anger. He leans down, whispering to Zeke, but clearly loud enough for me to hear. "I think someone's PMSing."

"I'm going to kill you, Ashton!" I shout at him as I chase him out of my room and into the hallway.

He takes a step back, retreating with Zeke in his arms.

"Everything okay?" Luca asks, stepping over boxes in the hallway that are labeled for the bathroom and hall closet. Clearly, the bathroom boxes weren't even put into the bathroom.

Luca doesn't have any clue about Ashton and me hooking up. I can't even categorize it as dating. We haven't officially gone out on a date. But we hang out together whenever we get the opportunity, which, in my mind, isn't often enough.

I'm hoping that'll change now that we live together.

Which sort of complicates matters, but it's no worse than Luca discovering the relationship between Ashton and me.

He can't find out.

Luca will kill Ashton.

At least he'll try to. I'm not sure Ashton won't have the upper hand and kick Luca's ass, or worse.

Ashton leaves me to do the talking. Standing in the hallway, he lifts Zeke into the air and pretends to drop him, which earns him a fit of giggles from the toddler.

"Your teammate is just being a jerk," I say.

Luca glances at Ashton. "Be nice to my sister. I know you two don't always get along, but there's plenty of room in this place not to murder each other. Okay?"

"She's the one starting fights," Ashton says, glaring at me. But I can see the hint of a smile playing under his lips. He's milking this fight, trying to make Luca believe we actually hate each other.

I don't know why my brother would think that, since I hang out around here often enough and watch movies with Ashton. But I do give him a ton of shit for the documentaries he plays. They're boring as hell, and I swear he does it to piss me off.

"I'm not sure the house is big enough with his ego," I quip.

"Truce," Luca demands, glancing between us. "Or I swear I'll make the two of you share a bedroom, with two beds, and keep you locked in there until classes resume."

"You're mean," I feign annoyance with Luca. "But fine. Truce." I hold out my hand to Ashton to shake on it.

Ashton begins to hold out a hand but pauses his

movements. "As long as I can still have girls in my room while she's in there, I don't care."

I yank my hand back and ball it into a fist.

"You're really risking your life," I threaten.

Luca scowls at Ashton. "He's joking. There will be no wild parties or countless girls coming into your room. We have Zeke here, who needs a normal life."

"Normal," Ashton says and raises an eyebrow, glancing at me. Nothing about our situation or circumstance is normal. "Right," he slowly draws out.

"Don't make me regret all of us moving in together," Luca says. It sounds like a threat, but none of this was up to him. His parents pulled the strings, like they always do.

Zeke squirms in Ashton's arms, growing restless, and he lifts him into the air, pretending to throw him, this time at Luca. "Catch?"

"Don't you dare throw my son!" Harper's voice emanates through the hallway.

"Just kidding," Ashton says. "Aren't we?" He nuzzles Zeke, who grabs at Ashton's nose.

Harper stalks her way past the boxes toward us. "Give him here," she says, holding out her arms for Zeke.

The moment Zeke sees his mama, he starts squirming for her and holds his arms out.

Ashton relinquishes his hold on the little boy, and I smirk proudly. "Good, now you can help with unpacking," I say.

Luca points at the boxes labeled *bathroom*. "Might as well get started, since you're finished in your bedroom."

"Can I help Nova unpack? She has a lot of boxes in her room," Ashton asks, but he's looking at me, waiting for my answer.

"No," Luca and I both say in unison.

"You're no fun," he mutters as he grabs the nearest *bathroom* box abandoned in the hallway and shoves it into the bathroom.

"It could be worse," I say. "Mom and Dad offered to help. We could have the entire mafia crew unpacking our things."

"And planting bugs," Harper quips, carrying Zeke with her back down the hallway.

"They wouldn't do that—right?" I ask, glancing at Luca and Ashton.

Ashton doesn't answer. He goes into the bathroom with the box and shuts the door.

I doubt he's unpacking, probably just sulking that I got him into trouble.

ELEVEN

MORENO

Knocking on Dante's office door, I've been inwardly debating my options.

Stewing over the truth isn't going to make it go away.

But I can't keep ignoring what I saw.

I won't.

Something must be done about it.

"Can I have a word with you, sir?" I steal Dante's attention for a beat, needing to talk with him.

I've waited too long as it is.

"Of course," he says and gestures for me to step into his office and have a seat.

Dante's brow furrows, and he loosens his tie. It's late, and while we should be closing up for the night, there's always more to do.

"That look on your face has *me* worried," Dante says.

His slight concern pales in comparison to the knot in my stomach.

I want to vomit, but that would be frowned upon, doing so in the mafia boss's office.

I exhale heavily and find the words that I've been desperately wanting to say, eating me alive inside.

"It's about the boy you hired and my daughter." I grit between clenched teeth. If I bite down any harder, I'm likely to crack a tooth.

Dante tilts his head to the side.

"The boy. Do you mean Ashton?" Dante asks and then narrows his eyes. "What makes you think anything is happening, Moreno?"

Dante is a good judge of character, not to mention

that he can read me better than anyone else under his command.

How he hasn't seen the stress and worry on my face, I suppose I've learned to hide some of my tells.

"I witnessed Ashton and my daughter sneaking into the hall closet together when he came to visit for Christmas."

Dante's eyes tighten and he leans back in his chair, clasping his hands together on his desk. He tilts his head back, thinking about my accusation.

"And you think something nefarious is going on under my roof?" Dante questions.

"I think he's fucking my little girl," I snap at the mafia boss.

Dante doesn't so much as flinch. "Nova is eighteen. She's off at college, living with this boy you worry about."

Heat licks my skin as I tug the top button of my shirt collar loose. I'm suffocating just thinking about his paws all over my daughter.

"I know," I choke out. I pinch the bridge of my nose

and then glare at Dante. "I blame you, for bringing him into our home, letting him work for the family."

Dante sighs.

He doesn't say a word, not at first.

He glances at his clasped hands and then at me.

"I might have an idea."

"You might have an idea?" Questioning the mafia boss isn't usually wise, but I can't stop myself.

Might doesn't satisfy me. I'm filled with an unbridled rage. If it were up to me, I'd have the man shacking up with my daughter killed or, at the very least, tortured and castrated.

But he works for Dante.

So do I.

While I've worked for the man longer, it doesn't make it any less of a complication.

"Do you trust me?" Dante asks, staring at me, gaze unwavering.

"Implicitly."

I wouldn't be doing this job if I didn't trust my boss. He's also my best friend, but sometimes his choices are skewed, like screwing Nikki at the bar that night, getting her pregnant.

Of course, he knew who she was—the daughter of his enemy—and he still went after her.

He didn't heed my advice when I told him to leave well enough alone.

"Good, because I have an idea, but you'll need to let me handle it."

I don't like being kept in the dark but agree all the same.

"I trust you," I say, and while it's the truth, I don't trust that snake Ashton who wants to steal my little girl's virginity.

TWELVE

NOVA

"Can I come in?" Ashton knocks on my open bedroom door, distracting me while reading a book.

I left my door open because Zeke keeps tearing down the hallway, knocking, running into my room for cuddles, and then running away.

It's his own version of peek-a-boo or some other toddler game that I haven't quite figured out yet.

He's a cute kid but makes me realize how deep Luca's gotten himself in with Harper.

They seem happy, at least from the outside, but

everyone in the house knows the truth. They don't have to hide it from any of us.

"Nova?" Ashton says when I don't answer him.

Like I have much of a choice? I know him, he's not going to leave until he annoys me with whatever he has to say.

"Yeah, come in." I wave him in and sit up and put a bookmark in my novel, closing the pages.

He shuts the door behind himself, and I raise a curious eyebrow.

I'm still annoyed about his lack of help with unpacking my room and the house this afternoon, but he eventually pitched in and now the boxes have all been unpacked and everything has been put away.

"Your room looks good," he says, glancing around, taking it all in.

"Don't expect a thank you," I say, glaring at him.

I hung up white string lights along the wall and a corkboard adorned with a handful of pictures of my friends.

There's still more for me to do to decorate my room, but I'm too tired tonight to finish it.

I stare at him, wondering why he's in here. It's certainly not to applaud my efforts for unpacking and putting away my stuff.

He wanders over to the photographs on my wall, studying them. "You're missing a picture."

"Am I?" I ask, watching him.

He doesn't know who my friends are or what pictures I brought with me from home. He never even stepped foot into my childhood bedroom back at home.

"You need one of your boyfriend," Ashton says.

My lips part, and I raise an eyebrow. We haven't quite put labels on whatever this thing is between us.

Hard to put a label like boyfriend on him when we haven't done anything outside of the house together.

"That'd be hard to do since my brother doesn't know about you. And we haven't even gone on a date yet. Boyfriend status doesn't come from bedroom activities alone."

"Then let's go out on a date," Ashton says. "Wednesday night, you, me, and dinner out."

"And what about Luca?"

Ashton frowns. "You want to invite your brother on our date? That's kinky."

I snort.

He's got quite the sense of humor. "No. How are you going to handle him finding out about us?" I ask.

It's why I hadn't let my thoughts linger into dating territory because, this fun thing between us, how can it last in secret?

Luca isn't going to be thrilled when he discovers we've been sleeping together. He made it clear to all of his teammates that I'm off-limits.

Just because I'm enrolled at Evergreen isn't going to change his stance on being my overprotective and overbearing older brother.

Ashton closes the distance between us, coming toward my bed where I'm seated. "We'll deal with it when the time comes."

"The entire team knows, Ashton."

He runs a hand through his hair. "They haven't said anything to him, and he's plenty distracted with the wedding next month. Let's just give it some more time."

I don't argue with him because I know Luca isn't going to take the news well. I really don't want to be on the receiving side of his wrath when he finds out.

Besides, the last thing I want is to ruin something that hasn't even fully gotten started yet. I want to see where this thing between me and Ashton leads. Especially if he's planning on taking me out.

Besides, there's a chance it could still fizzle out.

Why risk letting Luca in on what could be absolutely nothing?

I've been fantasizing about what a date with Ashton Rinaldi would be like, but that's as far as it had gone —a fantasy.

Until now.

"Wednesday, it's a date," I say and pat the mattress beside me. There isn't much room, but he can come hang out with me, keep me company for a bit.

It's not like I'm getting to sleep anytime soon.

I'm overstimulated and not the least bit capable of shutting my eyes and falling asleep.

And with Ashton near me, I find it even harder to relax.

His lips quirk up in a wayward smile. "Good. I can't wait." He flops down on the twin-sized bed with me and stretches out. "Your bed is super comfy."

"I know," I say cheekily. "I picked out the best mattress, so you'd be tempted to sleep in here with me."

"Really?" Ashton asks, his eyes widening.

I laugh, shaking my head, trying to hide the smile growing on my face. "No," I say.

He is far too gullible.

It's cute.

He rests a hand on my thigh and gives it a prominent squeeze.

My breath catches in my throat, and I try to pretend his touch doesn't turn me into a puddle of goo.

"Are you ready for classes Monday?" I ask,

attempting to distract him, and maybe I'm distracting myself too.

He chuckles. "Never. I live for hockey and our off days. What are you taking this semester?"

"All gen eds. Boring stuff." I climb off the bed and already miss his touch on my thigh. I grab my backpack, dig out my schedule and hand it to him to purview.

He glances it over, studying it intently. "We're both in Psychology 101."

"Great, they'll get to tell us what a basket case you are," I joke.

Ashton quips a smile. "Takes one to know one."

He hands me back my schedule, and I fold it and tuck it back into a side pocket of my backpack before climbing back onto the bed.

"Scoot over." I shove at him playfully. "You're hogging my bed."

The sly smile spreads farther across his face as he rolls onto his back, laying his head on my pillow, stretching out as he takes up the entire mattress. "Come and join me."

I playfully snarl at him as I pounce on him. I straddle his hips, my hands firmly planted against his chest. "I should punish you for what you did this afternoon."

He smirks up at me. "I'd like to see that; show me what you'd do to me."

I lean down, my breath teasing his lips as I grind my hips against his. He grips my hips and his head dips back, eyes closing. "If this is your idea of punishment, I'm a glutton for pain," Ashton rasps.

His voice is filled with lust, and it makes my insides tingle.

Rocking my hips against his drives my own body hotter, and I lean down, letting my breasts brush against him as I cover his lips with mine, needing a taste, craving him.

Ashton's hands remain steady on my hips while he grinds back up into me as I rock my hips against him. He raises his body up, his lips moving to that sweet spot on my neck as he begins sucking and kissing, making my insides melt.

"Fuck, Ashton," I mutter, realizing how quickly I'm losing control.

"Is that permission?" He smiles up at me and rolls us around, taking command.

"Yes," I rasp, finding my body responding to his touch as he quickly disrobes me of my jeans, sliding them down my hips and tossing them to the floor.

His mouth is on my thighs, and the room is sweltering. I move my hands to my hips, lifting my shirt and throwing it across the room.

"You didn't even wait for me," Ashton quips, and he's all smiles. "I like it when you take charge, but it's my turn to be in control."

My insides quiver at his words, and his mouth trails a warm path of kisses down my neck as he unclasps my bra, removing it before latching onto my breast.

His mouth and his tongue swirl over my nipple, his fingers deftly exploring my body.

I arch into him, his touch turning my body to molten lava. My fingers find the waistband of his sweats, my touch featherlight as I guide my hand to his shaft, touching him, needing him.

"Nova," he growls and rests a hand on my arm. "I didn't come in here to fuck you."

"But you're in here now, and I'm naked," I say.

"Not fully naked. Let me help with that." He hooks his fingers into my panties, sliding them down my hips in one smooth motion. "Much better."

His breath is against my skin, burning a path of kisses back up my thighs as he caresses my legs and moves higher toward his destination.

"You have too many clothes on," I say and try to sit up to reach his sweats, wanting him naked with me. "I want to feel all of you."

Ashton moves off me, and I whimper, but it's only for a quick moment while he throws his clothes off and climbs back above me.

"Where do you want to feel *all of me*? Here?" he asks, and his fingers tease my pussy lips before gliding his palm over my bottom. "Or here?"

My eyes widen, and I inhale sharply. "Definitely not my ass. That's not yours to touch." I swat his hand away.

Ashton grins and chuckles. "Are you sure? I promise it can feel fucking amazing," he whispers into my ear, and I shudder.

There's no way he doesn't recognize what he does to me. My body is entirely his for the taking.

"If you touch my ass, I'll fucking cut off your air supply, Ashton."

"Got it. I'll respect your boundaries," he says. His mouth descends back onto mine.

I relax into his touch, the kiss, my body melting against him and relaxing.

I trust him.

His hands graze over my hip and down between my thighs, spreading my legs for him.

His lips move down between my thighs, and I cover my mouth with my hand, being careful not to scream, trying to keep my moans tempered.

The bedroom door swings open without warning. "Nova, do you have a—"

Harper's eyes widen as she witnesses Ashton tongue-fucking me, and I hear the door slam abruptly shut behind her.

"Shit," I gasp.

THIRTEEN

ASHTON

I climb off Nova, grabbing my clothes and throwing my sweatpants on. "I'm sorry. I need to talk to her—stop her from telling Luca."

I tear out of the room, chasing after Harper before she can reveal to Luca what she just witnessed.

I manage to catch her in the hallway. Her eyes are wide, she's leaning against the wall, aghast. She's probably still processing what she saw between us.

Harper glances up, seeing me, and opens her mouth. Before she has time to give me a tongue-lashing, I grab her and drag her back into Nova's bedroom.

"What are you—" she asks, her words unfinished.

Harper is grinding her teeth, glaring at me as I open the bedroom door, and she relents and steps back into Nova's bedroom. "Fine," she grumbles at me.

Nova is buried under the sheets. Her clothes are still strewn across the floor.

Why didn't she get dressed? At least she's covered herself up.

I shut the door behind Harper, locking it long enough to make sure that no one else barges in.

"We need to talk," I say, my gaze fixated on Harper.

She looks perplexed by what she saw. We can't even pretend it wasn't exactly what it looked like.

There's no explanation for how naked Nova was and my tongue doing wild things to her.

Telling her we're both in Biology together would not only be a lie but absolute insanity.

She's not dumb enough to believe what we're doing is *studying*.

"How long?" she asks.

I bend down and toss Nova's clothes that are on the floor to her.

She slips her clothes back on under the bedsheets.

The fact that this isn't the first instance should make no difference. We could lie and tell her we got caught up in the moment, but the fact remains that she cannot say a word about it.

"Does it matter? You can't tell Luca," I say, staring at Harper, silently begging her to not betray us.

"You can't ask me to keep that kind of a secret from him."

I step closer, towering over her. "It's not your secret to tell."

It's a threat, a mild one. I'm not intending to kill her, but I will do whatever is necessary to keep Luca from finding out.

She exhales softly and glances from me to Nova. "You have to tell him," Harper says. "He's going to find out, eventually."

"Just give us time. Okay?" Nova asks. "We will tell him. I just, I need more time."

Harper's jaw is tight, and she rolls her lips together. "I won't say anything tonight, but you can't ask me to keep this from him forever."

"It won't be forever," I assure her and rest a hand on her arm. "We just need more time."

Harper is silent for a beat, contemplating her options. "You owe me," she says, and I hate knowing that I owe anyone any favors, but I nod all the same.

"Deal."

FOURTEEN

ASHTON

Harper keeps our secret. She seems to avoid me for the next few weeks, and Nova and I are extra careful around the house to not seem overly affectionate.

We still watch television together in the living room, and our flirting is quite a bit tamer than it is in the bedroom when we're together in the house.

We've been out on a handful of dates, but between practice and studying, we haven't had too much free time. Not to mention, my weekends are booked at her parents' house, which has seemed a bit more tense than usual.

Moreno has been glaring at me at every opportunity, and Dante seems displeased with something I've done recently. I'm not sure exactly what I've done to piss them both off.

I've been helping Luca at the shooting range, perfecting his skill and working on his aim, which has taken a lot longer than I first anticipated.

"Ashton, can I have a word with you?" Dante asks.

Luca glances peculiarly at his father but doesn't interrupt or stop him.

"Of course, sir," I say and follow Dante down the maze of hallways to his office. He's asked me to keep tabs on Harper, make sure that she's keeping the family's secret.

"Come inside. Have a seat." He gestures to the empty chair across from his desk.

I sit, unsure what I'm doing in here. "Is everything okay, sir?" I ask.

"Yes, and no," Dante says. He closes the door, making sure it's just the two of us, alone.

"Harper hasn't told anyone about you, the family, or

the business," I say, making it clear that I've been doing my job as assigned.

It's why I keep showing up for lunch with Harper and Kensley. It's not because I like Kensley, although, for a beat, I thought she might have been catching feelings for me. But I'm pretty sure she's been giving off friend vibes recently.

"Good. I knew you would ensure our secret would remain safe," Dante says. "But that isn't why I asked you into my office."

I don't have the faintest idea what might be troubling Dante if it's not Harper. She seems to be the main cause of the Ricci family drama lately.

"Is it my father?" I ask. Dante and Aurelio talk somewhat regularly, I've been told.

Dante has been sharing stories of my involvement with the Ricci family business, keeping my father informed of my strengths and weaknesses, apparently.

I got an earful from my old man last week.

"This has nothing to do with Aurelio—your father,"

Dante says. "It's actually a much more sensitive subject."

Dante comes to perch himself at the edge of the desk, sitting in front of me, staring down at me.

"What I'm going to tell you, Ashton, it requires absolute discretion."

"Of course," I say and straighten up. "You have my loyalty, sir." While I will serve my father's business after graduation, right now I'm training, and my allegiance is to Dante Ricci.

Had our fathers not been allies, this would be quite a precarious situation.

"Good, I'm glad to hear that, son," he says. "Because I have a job for you. One that I've already spoken with your father about."

"Oh? What kind of assignment?" I ask, leaning forward, excitement bubbling inside of me.

Will I get my first mission to help take down an enemy of Dante's?

Is he going to want me to execute someone for him?

Perhaps he needs me to go undercover and spy on his enemy. It wouldn't be the first time he's asked me to keep tabs for him, but at least Harper was an easy assignment. Getting close to her hasn't been too problematic.

"It involves something a little more personal, a little less dark," Dante says. "And the pay—it will be an ongoing assignment and will include a hefty upfront payment along with a decent monthly stipend."

It sounds a bit too good to be true, but I trust him.

"Whatever it is, I'll do it."

"I'm glad you said that, because I need you to marry Harper McKenna," Dante says.

The air rushes out of my lungs, and I can't breathe.

He wants me to marry Harper?

He can't be serious, but the look on his face, he's not smiling and certainly not joking. There's no laughter bubbling out of him, no hint of humor.

And I've already agreed to it before even hearing his request.

I've never betrayed a don, but he can't honestly believe that Harper will agree to the arrangement.

Harper and Luca have been hooking up.

There's clearly a spark between them. There has been since the moment I saw the two of them together. They're either red-hot or ice-cold, and right now, the steam seems to be turned up between those two.

It's impossible not to hear them between the thin walls, especially when I'm in the living room on the sofa, watching a movie.

Luca will end me if I intervene in their relationship.

Of course, Dante killing me isn't a much better solution.

My life still ends in death.

I'd rather go up against Luca than his father and the entire Ricci family.

"And if she says no?" I ask, my throat raw.

I don't want to marry Harper.

Yes, I had feelings for her when we first met, but

those desires fizzled out the moment I realized Luca really liked her.

And now there's Nova, the one girl who steals my breath away with a single glance. The one girl who I want to get to know every inch of, day in and day out.

It's hard enough keeping *her* a secret, but to even contemplate marrying Harper sets my nerves ablaze.

"Harper won't say no, because you won't let her. You're smart, son, you'll make sure she knows marrying you will be saving her life and her little boy's."

Working for the mafia is dangerous. I've never been blind to it, but knowing that I'm about to push an idea of a wedding onto a girl who isn't interested in me, while having feelings for someone else, I'm physically sick.

Dante reaches for his knife on the desk, his fingers grazing the blade.

It's a silent warning.

Obey or death.

He threatened Harper's life once and Luca's. It wouldn't take much for him to order my death.

I'm nothing to him, just another soldier.

But what worries me most of all, he might even hurt Zeke.

"You don't have an issue following an order, do you?" Dante asks.

FIFTEEN

HARPER

January and February are filled with snow and cold. I've gotten into a routine with Zeke, taking him to daycare on campus every day while I'm in class.

Luca and I don't have any classes together this semester, which is a bummer, but I'm also not sweating another economics class, which is a relief.

I managed to pass my final last semester, all thanks to Luca's help studying throughout the entire semester. I've also kept my GPA up to continue my scholarship, which is at least one thing that I don't have to worry about.

Fitting into my wedding dress, however, is a new fear I've unlocked.

It took until the third time the seamstress made alterations to get it right.

His mom didn't attend the latest fitting, and to be honest, I was relieved because it meant I didn't have to put on a fake smile about the whole ordeal.

Not that she doesn't know the truth.

But I've been trying to act cheery and excited, not wanting to worry her that I'll flake at the absolute last minute.

Planning a wedding is supposed to be the most exciting part, but I haven't done anything to plan the wedding. I've been a bystander.

I got to pick out my wedding dress; that was the most involvement that I've had.

And I suppose I got to pick the date, in February.

The choices don't even feel like they're really mine.

Luca has been distant, busy with his father on weekends, at practice and the gym during the weekdays, not to mention his hockey games.

He hasn't tried to be distant, at least I don't think so, it's just trying to mesh our lives together and with Zeke. I can't help but wonder if he still hasn't forgiven me for lying to him.

There's a prominent knock at the bedroom door. "Come in," I call out as I try to secure my wedding gown.

Zeke is still at daycare for another hour before I have to swing by and pick him up.

Luca is in class. I'm not sure who's home right now.

I'm trying on my gown, staring at my reflection in the full-length mirror.

"Wow," Ashton's voice catches me off-guard, and I spin around in the gown, holding it up, but it's not about to fall down. It's a zipper back, making it easier than having to cinch it closed. While I loved the design of the corset, I felt like I was suffocating.

Another alteration.

While it gives the illusion of a corset in the back, there's a hidden zipper to make the gown more comfortable.

Somehow, the dress is ready for the wedding this Saturday.

I kept hoping that if it hadn't been ready, then perhaps the wedding would be postponed.

"Too much?" I ask, feeling his eyes move over the gown.

He shakes his head. A wry smile cracks his features.

"Not at all."

I bunch up the bottom, keeping the train from getting trampled on. "What's up?" I ask, wondering why he's knocking on my door in the afternoon and not at the gym with Luca.

"I wanted to talk to you. I have a proposition," Ashton says, and I pinch my lips together, not liking the way this is sounding.

My displeasure must be obvious because he forces a smile.

"Relax," Ashton holds up his hands in surrender. "I'm just trying to help you."

I don't trust his version of *help*.

"Help me?" I raise an eyebrow skeptically. "I don't think you're in the business of helping anyone, Ashton."

He was there the night that I encountered the little boy.

I didn't see him trying to help anyone but himself.

"I don't think you should marry Luca. You should marry me instead."

I nearly die of laughter.

Ashton can't be serious.

My eyes water as the giggles spill out, until I realize he's not laughing or making a joke.

"You're crazy. Besides, his father insisted I marry Luca, his son would be mafia, I would be protected." I wave my hand precariously through the air as if that explains away the last few months of chaos.

"His father has made other arrangements. He wants us to wed."

"I don't believe you," I say and take a step back. "And you're dating Nova!" I shake my head, feeling betrayed for all of us —Luca, Nova, and myself.

Ashton's tone isn't any less quiet or filled with any bit of remorse. "This wasn't my idea."

I can see the storm in his eyes, the conflicting emotions swirling across his face, his shoulders slumped, filled with defeat.

He's not convincing me, and he's certainly not in love with me.

"Then that's a wonderful reason for the two of us to get hitched, because it wasn't your idea," I snap.

I reach for the zipper on my gown, wanting to rip it off. The thought of marrying anyone right now has my blood boiling and I'm finding it hard to breathe.

"Turn around!" I scold him as I loosen the material, find the zipper, and let it slink to the ground.

Ashton obeys, turning to the door, facing away from me.

I step out of the wedding dress, grabbing a robe and slipping it on quickly, not wanting to be undressed in his presence.

"We aren't marrying. I don't even know what's gotten into you," I say.

He continues to face the door, giving me more than enough privacy, not realizing that I'm done dressing. "Trust me, it wasn't my idea. I'm falling for Nova."

"Then why would you suggest that we get married!" I can't stop myself from shouting at him. Thankfully, no one else is home, or everyone would have heard me.

He chances a glance over his shoulder and when he realizes I'm dressed, he turns to face me.

"Dante demanded I marry you instead of Luca. He wants you, a loose end, tied up and doesn't want you destroying his son's life."

"Wow," I say, not sure if those are Ashton's words or Dante's.

The wedding planning has been going on for months.

Why now?

Why the sudden change?

Does Luca know?

"What the hell happened, Ashton?" I step closer,

prepared to beat the answer out of him if I have no other choice.

"Nova's father found out about me and his daughter," Ashton says. "I think this is his way of keeping me away from her."

It's a punishment.

For all of us.

I tilt my head back, staring at the ceiling, running my hands frustratedly through my hair. "I'm not marrying you!"

"Fine, but Dante isn't going to be happy when you walk down the aisle and it's his son who's waiting for you."

"Well, fuck him! I'm—" I shut my mouth before I say anything incriminating.

"You're what?" Ashton asks, shaking his head, waiting for me to elaborate.

"I'm fucking tired of being told what to do," I grumble and point at the door. "Get out of my bedroom!"

Ashton stalks to the door, throws it open, and glances at me over his shoulder. "Dante isn't going to be pleased."

"That makes two of us!"

————

I'm in bed early, after Zeke is sound asleep. The warm bed calls to me and I willingly oblige. Had it been earlier in the day, I'd have taken a nap, but it's just after nine and I can't seem to keep my eyes open.

I barely drift to sleep when I hear the bedroom door creak open, and I glance up, relieved to see it's Luca and not Zeke sneaking out of bed.

Having him go from a crib to a big boy bed has been hellacious. He keeps escaping his room after I put him down, refusing to go to bed until he tires me out.

"Sorry, didn't mean to wake you," Luca says as he stumbles in the darkness, fumbling through the dresser before giving up.

"It's okay, I don't mind."

I watch as he disrobes, his clothes in a pile on the

floor, removing everything before climbing into bed with me.

This is a pleasant surprise.

"Come here," he mumbles, pulling me against him and his arms wrap around my waist, holding me close.

"You're naked," I rasp, stating the obvious as I let my hand glide across his bare skin, grazing his hip and then slowly letting my hand wander down his stomach.

"I couldn't find my boxers," Luca says. "Did you rearrange the drawers again?"

I chuckle against his chest.

"What's so funny?"

"I don't think you've done laundry for a week, maybe two. All your dirty clothes are in the hamper in the closet, including your boxers."

Luca curses and then kisses my forehead. "Laundry tomorrow."

I'm glad he's not climbing out of bed now to start a load.

My fingers caress his skin, sliding across his hip to his back, feeling over his ass. "I like it when you're in bed with me, naked."

Luca grins and plants a soft kiss on my lips. "That's my line, babe."

"Too bad we can't share it." I pull him against me, rolling onto my back, wanting to feel his body against me.

"Oh, I think there's plenty to share." His lips are warm and inviting, his body heating my very core as I sink farther into the mattress as he presses into me.

I drink him in, every kiss another sweet taste of honey and almonds as I nip at his neck. "You smell really good," I whisper between kisses as I nuzzle his neck.

Luca pulls back. "I used your shampoo at practice. You're just smelling yourself, babe."

"I don't think so." I shake my head. "Definitely smells better on you."

His hands glide down my hips, finding the hem of my tank top, teasing against the skin as I squirm under his ministrations. "You like that," he whispers, memorizing every detail about me.

"I like you," I say, my cheeks flooding with heat as he studies me like I'm his next exam.

He guides my tank top over my head but doesn't fully remove it as he tangles my hands together, binding them with the cotton material. He keeps one hand forcefully on my arms, pinning me down.

"I *really* like having you like this," Luca whispers into my ear, and a shudder courses through my body. "I knew you'd like it too."

My nipples pebble against him, my insides throbbing from just the mere act of being completely at his mercy.

"I do," I whisper, letting him know that I'm giving him consent. I'd let him do almost anything to me, willingly. I trust him that much.

"Good girl," Luca whispers into my ear, and my body floods with heat, and my eyes momentarily close as I let myself give in to temptation.

I wrap my legs around him and lift my hips against the mattress, needing contact, wanting to grind against him for a little indulging before the main course.

My heart races and my insides tingle.

"It drives me wild when you give yourself to me completely," Luca says. His mouth hovers over mine, and I raise up, craving another taste.

I can't stand all the teasing. I need more.

He makes me feel so damn desperate, like I can't ever get enough when I'm with him.

He keeps me trapped against the mattress, my arms above my head. "Don't move your hands," he instructs.

I nod, following his command.

"Good girl," he says with a knowing grin and flips me around, keeping my arms above me but my stomach against the mattress.

He slides my panties down my legs.

I feel exposed.

Vulnerable.

But I trust Luca.

"God, you're so fucking gorgeous," Luca whispers, and then I feel his tongue on my spine, the heat of his lips and mouth as he moves across my back, dropping kisses over my flesh.

Every place he marks feels scorched as I tremble, my hands clasped tight, bound above.

"Don't fight it," Luca whispers. "I want to see you come in all the different ways possible."

I whimper; his breath, his words, they're enough to make my insides turn from a warm tingle to a dull throb, craving contact.

"Are you going to fuck me?" I ask, my voice betraying me as I sound throaty and raw.

"Only if you ask nicely," Luca says, and his lips nibble on my hip. One hand holds my hands above my head, the other moves down to my folds as I spread my legs, and my God, the man knows how to work those fingers.

"Fuck," I mutter, widening my legs, wanting him to satisfy the dull ache.

I swear I can hear the smile on his face. "You are so perfect for me," Luca whispers, and I whimper when I feel the contact disappear from my hands. "Don't move," he commands.

Glancing over my shoulder, I see that he's shifting on the bed, guiding my hips up as he stares at my ass, or maybe it's my pussy he's admiring.

"Get a good enough look?" I glare at him, and he chuckles.

"Not even close. I just love every part of you," Luca admits, and a long finger glides over my bottom hole.

"What are you—" He grazes the skin but doesn't sink his finger in. "I want to claim you here."

My breath catches in my throat, nervous, my stomach a flurry of butterflies. "I've never—"

"Not tonight," he says, and his fingers circle my bottom as I squirm, unsure if he's going to push past my little hole or just tease me until oblivion, making me both excited but nervous. "When we're married."

He shifts on the mattress, guiding his head between my legs and then lowers me down as his tongue swipes out, licking my pussy, tasting my juices as he thrusts his tongue into my wetness.

I know I'm already dripping for him, the evidence on his tongue as he laps at my arousal, his tongue moving from my folds up to my clit.

With each swipe of his tongue, I grow restless. I loosen the restraints from my tank top and slip my hands free, tangling my fingers in his hair, needing to touch him, to feel him, to have some semblance of control.

My pussy throbs, needing more than just his tongue.

I can't reach his cock, and I whimper in protest. "I want to fuck you," I whine, letting my fingers stroke his hair and move down his neck.

He releases his grip on my hips and moves his mouth to my inner thigh, taking a playful nip as I squeal at him and smack him away.

"No biting down there!" I growl, but he didn't hurt me.

He startled me.

Luca smiles and pulls me above him, my body

crashing onto his. "By all means, I'd never deny you any pleasure, ever."

"Of course, you wouldn't when it involves your pleasure too." I grin and then climb down his body, my thumb teasing the head of his cock as I watch his eyes struggle to remain open.

He's watching intently as I bend down and drag my tongue up his shaft.

His fingers tangle in my hair as I let my tongue swirl over the head and then bring my lips down his length, taking him into my mouth.

"Yes, just like that." His voice is rough and raw, filled with lust.

I swear I hear him growl.

"Keep doing that," he rumbles as I feel the first taste of wetness glisten from the head.

His hand fingers my hair, gripping me tighter as I take him deeper into my throat. "You take it so well."

I stare up, my eyes glistening as he struggles to keep his gaze on me.

He's close and yanks me away, gasping for breath, panting hard, as he struggles to calm down.

He reaches for the bedside table, grabbing a condom from inside, tearing the foil packet open and putting it on.

Luca's hands are on my hips as I guide his shaft inside of me, and holy hell, does he feel fucking amazing.

My hands claw at his chest, stroking down the skin as I move my hips against his with each slow and drawn out thrust.

"You feel so fucking amazing," Luca rasps.

My head dips back, body arching as I ride him, grinding my clit against him, making my body begin the first wave as I tremble in his arms.

Luca lifts his hips, matching my intensity as my insides clench and spasm on his cock.

"Fuck yes, come for me, Harper," he chants, and I swear my body is on fire, ready to explode.

The moan roars through me, my toes curling and insides trembling, tightening down, taking everything he has to offer as I arch into the orgasm.

Luca moves his hips with mine, sitting up to face me, his movements hardly slowing as he grinds and thrusts his hips against mine.

Fuck.

What I thought was a decent orgasm is a million times more intense as it tears through every inch of my body, like a star exploding in the darkest night.

Luca stares straight into my soul, and his lips capture mine, silencing the pleasurable scream that rips through me.

His body tightens against me, and I keep my hips grinding, moving faster and harder, knowing exactly what he craves.

Gasping for breath, my lips tease his ear. "Come for me, Luca," I rasp. "You feel so fucking incredible."

He's close, and the growl that emanates from the back of his throat tells me he's nearly there.

Luca's mouth covers mine, pushing his tongue inside past my lips, drinking me in, stealing my breath away as his body tightens and shudders, spilling himself inside of me.

My heart pounds wildly against my chest, and finally untangling, I lie back on the mattress while he tosses the condom into the nearby wastebasket.

Luca collapses beside me, gasping for air. "Damn, you're going to kill me."

The sly smile spreads across my face. "You're the one who came to bed naked."

"It was so fucking worth it," Luca says. He pulls me into his arms as I lie with my back against his chest.

"Your heart is going to pound out of your chest," I whisper, feeling it beating against his ribcage.

"You do that to me," he whispers, kissing my shoulder. "I'm the luckiest guy alive."

"Why's that?" I glance back at him, smiling. My body is humming and ablaze from the heat between us.

Luca's fingers caress my waist, his touch featherlight. "Because I get to marry you."

It isn't long before Luca's soft breath tickles my neck. He doesn't move, his grip on me relaxes, but his hold doesn't loosen.

I can't sleep.

It's not for lack of trying.

Reluctantly, I untangle from his embrace, careful not to startle him.

I grab my clothes from the floor, my tank top and panties. Then I reach for his sweats because I don't have any pajama bottoms nearby.

I slip on his pants. He won't care, or even notice for that matter. I'm quiet as I patter out of the bedroom, careful not to wake him.

I head into the kitchen, grabbing a glass of water. I'm parched and drink the entire glass in one shot. I grab the pitcher in the fridge to refill my water glass and hear footsteps behind me.

One swift glance over my shoulder, and I see it's Ashton.

He's wearing sweats and a white t-shirt that clings to his body. His hair is ruffled, like he's been running his fingers roughly through the ends, or maybe Nova has been—best not to ask.

"Can't sleep?" I guess, assuming that's why he's awake and joining me in the kitchen.

"Not with the sounds you were making," Ashton says, startling me.

I take another sip, hoping to cool off my rosy cheeks.

"Shit. You heard that?"

"The whole neighborhood heard you two."

Ashton steps closer, invading my personal space.

"You must really be trying to convince Luca you love him with a performance like that," he says.

"It wasn't a performance."

His eyes tighten as he studies me. "I don't believe you."

I take another sip of water. "I don't care what you believe. It doesn't matter to me."

Luca knows that what we have is real. I don't have to convince *him*.

"Come on, Harper. You don't have to lie to me. You were *really loud* back there." Ashton gestures toward my bedroom. "A girl doesn't make those kinds of sounds unless she's trying really hard to sound convincing."

"Your best friend rocked my world," I say, staring Ashton dead in the eye. "Not that it's any of your damn business."

Ashton leans back against the counter. "I'm just saying, the offer still stands about the wedding. There's still time to choose—"

"Are you seriously suggesting I marry you?" Why is he bringing up this asinine idea again?

"You don't have to decide until the wedding day," Ashton says.

"I'm not marrying you, Ashton. I don't even like you very much."

"Ouch." He holds a hand up to his heart. "I'm just trying to save Luca, help him out."

I take a step back, bumping into the refrigerator. I don't see how him offering to marry me is helping Luca at all. "How do you figure?"

"Come on, Luca never wanted kids. He only offered to marry you to protect you from his father."

"And what you're doing is so different?" I glare at Ashton. "You have a girlfriend!"

He throws his hand up, a finger against his lips, warning me to keep it quiet.

It's not like I said who his girlfriend was, but Nova wouldn't be happy with me if I married her boyfriend. "Is this your way of breaking it off with her, Ashton? Because that's a really shitty way to end a relationship."

Ashton steps closer. "Keep your voice down," he whispers. "And, no. I really like *her.*"

I thought I was being relatively quiet, but I nod, agreeing not to wake the entire house. The last person I want to wake is Zeke. It'll take me forever to put him back down to bed, and he's already going to be up at the crack of dawn.

"Then quit hitting on me and go to bed," I snap, pointing in the direction of his bedroom.

"I'm trying to help you, but clearly, you can't see that. Luca likes you, he'd do anything for you, but are you going to tie him down with a family when he's not in love with you?"

I clench my jaw, my lips pursed as I glare at Ashton.

He's not making his case.

It's not like Ashton and I are in love.

"Dante agreed that if I marry you, you'll be safe. He'll leave you and Zeke alone."

"And what about Luca? Will he still be forced to work for his father?" That's the only leverage that I still have—trying to break Luca out of his father's clutches, granting him freedom.

"Dante isn't going to just let his son be free from the responsibilities of the family. Come on, the odds of Luca even getting drafted are next to nothing. It's nearly impossible, given his stats. He's a great player, but he's not professional material. It's why his father agreed to the NHL as an exception clause. He doesn't think he'll make it to any professional team."

"And you?" I ask, staring at Ashton. "Do you think he'll make it to the NHL?"

Ashton's shoulders slump. "I think it's a fantasy. He can certainly try to enter the draft, but getting to play pro, it's what we all dream about."

"I'm not marrying you," I reiterate. I finish the last sip of water and place my empty glass in the sink.

"I could convince Dante to pay for your son's education and anything Zeke needs if you follow through with marrying me."

"You can't buy me, Ashton. I'm not for sale."

"What's going on?" Luca's voice vibrates through the kitchen as he stalks in, looking sexy and sleepy, all at the same time. He's at least wearing sweats, although not the ones from today since I stole them from him.

He probably grabbed a pair from the dirty clothes pile.

My gaze is on his bare chest, though, and I can't seem to look away. Every muscle in his body ripples ferociously.

"Just heading to bed," Ashton says, attempting to head past Luca.

Luca grabs Ashton by the shirt, stopping him from passing. "What was that about buying my girlfriend?" he growls at his best friend.

I rest a hand on Luca's arm, trying to calm him down. "Your father is just trying to interfere in our wedding. Don't worry," I say, placing a soft kiss on his lips.

He reluctantly lets go of Ashton, releasing his hold on him, but he doesn't let him leave the kitchen, blocking his exit.

Luca glares at Ashton and then stares at me. "That doesn't make me feel any better, learning that Dante is meddling. Tell me what's going on," Luca demands.

SIXTEEN

LUCA

My bed feels lonely this morning, and I awaken at dawn, which is far too early. I reach for my phone; there's no new messages yet from Harper.

Harper and I agreed that the night before the wedding, we'd spend it apart. I'd stay at my parents, and she'd come up with Kensley and Zeke on Saturday morning.

I offered to pick her up, but she insisted that she wanted us to follow the tradition of the groom not seeing the bride before the wedding.

I never knew Harper was superstitious.

It seems there's a lot to learn about her. And while I've been doing my best not to keep her at a distance, we haven't exactly seen each other much lately.

That's both of our fault.

Harper has been busy with schoolwork and her son, Zeke.

Zeke is a full-time job when it comes to evenings and weekends. When I do get the chance to spend a few minutes curled up on the sofa with Harper, Zeke is always stealing her attention from me.

I never knew I'd have to compete with a two-year-old for attention.

But I get it, Zeke is her son. I'm trying not to feel jealous, but sometimes it's hard when she spends more time with him than me.

That's not all on her. I've been busy with the hockey team, my father's business, and schoolwork.

I hate that we don't have any classes together this semester. Our schedules are all over the place, in opposite directions on campus. There's no walking her to class this semester, not that I don't want to, but

I haven't been able to find the time. I can't be in two places at once.

I've tried spending a bit more time with Zeke, but he's always choosing his mama over me.

Not that I blame the kid, she is a prettier choice.

She always knows how to make him laugh.

I love his laughter. It actually makes me think that one day, maybe we could have a kid of our own, a little sibling for Zeke.

But not today.

After college.

When we're both ready for that type of commitment.

The marriage thing is enough to jump into headfirst when we're both not ready.

But I'm doing it for *her*.

Every waking moment, I'm thinking about Harper, wondering if I can truly keep her and Zeke safe from my father, from the world out there.

I may even be falling in love with her, but I'm not sure.

I've never actually been in love.

I've lusted after girls, but love, I can't say I know one hundred percent what that feels like.

But I can safely say that I'm in the blossoming stages of love. That without Harper, I would feel empty. And that while I'm nervous as hell about our wedding today, I know without a doubt that I'm doing the right thing.

I need to keep her and Zeke safe.

I glance at my cell phone. The last text from Harper was last night, when she texted me, *Goodnight. See you tomorrow.*

It's a simple text. There was even a heart emoji, which brought a smile to my face because the girl has a way of making my heart soar.

Love, though, I'm not sure.

I'm definitely falling for her.

Without a doubt, I'm happy that she's the girl I'll be marrying. If it had to be someone, I'd rather it be Harper.

I force myself out of bed, knowing it's going to be a long day. Hopefully, a good one.

I text Harper. She's probably busy with Zeke this morning, or if she's lucky, she's still asleep.

Can't wait to see you, wifey.

I hit send and then regret the choice of *wifey*.

I'm teasing her.

Being playful.

I hope she sees it that way and doesn't get nervous.

It's too late, the text is already sent.

There's no read receipt yet, so I pull on a pair of sweats and a t-shirt and head downstairs to grab breakfast and much-needed coffee.

I don't exactly need the jolt of caffeine with the way my heart is already galloping, but it's the familiar that I'm craving, and without Harper here this morning, it'll have to do.

Ashton spent the night last night, and though I want to hate him for trying to steal my girlfriend, I'm angrier at Dante.

My best friend never would have suggested marrying Harper if Dante hadn't given him an order, and Ashton is all about following the chain of command.

Well, fuck Dante.

I'm marrying Harper.

Last night, Ashton offered to take me to a strip club for my bachelor party, but the thought of a strange woman grinding against me, dancing provocatively, didn't stir any hint of desire.

Unless that girl is Harper, but Kensley spent the night over at our house, and there was zero chance Harper was going to show up at the compound and give me a lap dance and strip show.

So, we spent the evening hanging out, drinking and swapping stories.

Moreno and Dante joined us for beers around nine o'clock last night, the mood much more chipper than I might have expected with those two.

And while I'd love to have snuck up from behind and slit Dante's throat for fucking with my love life, I give props to the man for actually giving a shit about me.

I suppose there's a first for everything.

But that was last night, and now the house is relatively quiet as the sun rises over the horizon.

Sleeping in wasn't going to happen this morning, not with thoughts of the wedding and Harper flickering through my mind.

I left my phone upstairs on the bed. If Harper texts me, I won't see it.

Dread is like a giant stone in my stomach, worried that something might happen to her on the way over.

I want to pick her up, drive her here, to know that she's safe, but she insisted that we don't see one another until we walk down the aisle.

I fucking hate that she's superstitious, but it's just a few hours until we're married.

Mr. and Mrs. Ricci.

She will take my last name.

The sound of it makes my heart beat faster.

I pour myself a cup of coffee, and Ashton comes stumbling down the hallway toward the kitchen.

"Morning," Ashton mutters, half-asleep.

He looks about how I feel, like he didn't get enough sleep.

I kept having dreams about the wedding, about Zeke, about Harper, and the mafia. I felt as though I didn't sleep at all, but I'm sure I managed a few hours of shuteye.

I sip my coffee and step aside so Ashton can grab himself a mug.

"Do you know if Harper's parents will be at the wedding?" Ashton asks.

I frown, unsure why he's asking me about her parents. "I'm not sure. I don't think she knows. She mentioned to me the other night that she left them a message, but they didn't call her back."

"They didn't RSVP?" he asks.

I rub the back of my neck. "Mom dealt with the RSVPs, so I'm unsure."

"Your mom planned your wedding?" Ashton smirks, pouring his mug of coffee. "Wow. You really are a mama's boy."

"I'm going to kill you," I growl, lunging at him, and Dante stalks out from the basement and rounds the corner into the kitchen, hearing me.

"You won't," Dante says matter-of-factly. "You two ought to be getting along." He wraps one arm around my shoulder and the other around Ashton's.

I swear my father sees Ashton more and more as a son. Probably why he suggested that Ashton marry Harper.

My shoulders tense with his arm around me. Everything about it is unnatural.

"It's going to be quite a day this afternoon with the wedding. I'm looking forward to it," Dante says, and a wry smile crosses his face.

I just bet he's looking forward to it, thinking Ashton will marry Harper instead of me.

Fuck Dante.

I force a smile, not letting him know that I'm well

aware of his conniving little plan. I'd rather see the look of horror when Harper and I exchange vows.

I'll be fucking gleeful, just to spite my father.

Ashton looks slightly aghast and puts his mug that he just poured down on the counter. At least I know he hasn't told my father that he's spilled his secret to me.

Dante wouldn't be so forgiving. Probably why Ashton will keep his mouth shut. He's smart enough to know not to piss off the don, especially on the morning of his son's wedding.

Dante forces a smile before wandering out of the kitchen. "Stay out of trouble, you two, and no killing anyone before the wedding."

Ashton mutters something that sounds like a threat to Dante, which surprises the hell out of me, but maybe he's still cursing me for threatening him.

I ignore it as I sip my coffee and watch as he takes his mug and pours it down the sink.

"It'll be fine," I say, staring at Ashton.

"Yeah, well, I just lost my appetite," he grumbles.

I sip my coffee, the extra boost of adrenaline keeping me alert after a tough night's sleep without Harper beside me.

I never realized how much I'd depend on anyone else, and I don't dare want to admit it, but I'm falling in love with her.

There are worse things in the world than loving the person you're about to marry.

———

I'm dressed in my tux at my father's insistence. I'd have been fine wearing a suit to the wedding. The tuxedo is a bit confining. It doesn't help that I had to give measurements, but I didn't actually try it on until today.

It fits, better than I thought, but it doesn't mean I'm comfortable in it, either.

Ashton is keeping me company as I glance at my cell phone, yet again.

"Still nothing from Harper," I say.

My stomach is doing that tumbling motion, and I loosen the bow tie, finding it constricting.

I need to breathe.

I hurry toward a window, opening it, letting the cold February breeze into the bedroom.

"Give me that," Ashton says, taking my phone away from me.

"What if she tries to get ahold of me?" I glare at him, reaching for my phone as he shoves it behind his back.

"I'm sure she's already here, probably getting her gown on or her makeup done." Ashton is the voice of reason.

We're less than an hour until we're supposed to be walking down the aisle.

"Can you please go check?" I'm crawling out of my skin with worry.

I haven't heard a peep from Zeke. He hasn't even barged into the bedroom playing his own variation of hide and seek.

Although Harper is probably keeping that from happening after what she witnessed under my parents' roof.

"Yeah, just stay here. Okay?" Ashton tells me, and I nod, chewing on my bottom lip with worry.

My bedroom faces the courtyard, which means I can't even see when Harper would arrive, not that she has a car.

She insisted on taking the bus.

I should have driven her, screw silly superstitions. At least I'd know she's safe.

Ashton is gone for a while.

Too long if you ask me.

It leaves me with too many thoughts, and he still has my phone, so I can't even text her that I'm worried since I haven't heard from her.

Grimacing, I don't want to be controlling and overbearing, like Dante. I swore I'd never become my father, never have kids, never wed.

Staring at my reflection in the mirror, I'm afraid of the man I'm becoming.

Five minutes turns to ten.

I want to tear the entire compound apart looking for Harper, but it takes great restraint to stay in my bedroom. If she's wandering around the house, I don't want to run into her.

Well, I do, but I'm trying to respect her wishes.

I glance at the clock. We're nearing twenty minutes since Ashton went looking for Harper.

That rock in my stomach is turning into a boulder.

Ashton hasn't come back, but maybe he's helping Harper with Zeke. I can't imagine the little one is thrilled with sitting still long enough to put on fancy clothes.

There's a soft rap at the door.

"Come in."

Silently, I'm praying it's Harper.

The doorknob turns, and Kensley sneaks into my room. She's dressed in dark purple with black lace trim along the hemline. The dress looks nice on her, and the fact she's here means Harper must be, too, because they came together on the bus.

I breathe a sigh of relief.

"You're here."

Because if Kensley is here, then Harper is getting ready, hidden in another room, probably my mother's, making last-minute preparations to walk down the aisle.

"I am," Kensley says. Her eyes shine, but I feel like she's holding something back.

She has a folded slip of paper in her hands.

"Are those the vows?" I ask, glancing at her hands, wondering why she has them, unless she's holding them for Harper so they don't get lost or forgotten. "Can I see them?" I ask, knowing that I shouldn't, but I hadn't written any vows. It wasn't something that we'd talked about, but with twenty minutes until the start of the wedding, I'm slowly beginning to panic.

Truthfully, I've been panicking all morning, worried about Harper.

But seeing Kensley has eased those fears.

"Did you write vows?" Kensley asks, keeping the paper in her hands.

She's not handing it over to me.

Can't say I'm surprised. She is Harper's best friend. She'd do anything for her.

The nervous butterflies are back, but at least the boulder seems to have shrunk immensely. "I'm guessing I should have. Can I take a peek?"

Kensley steps farther into the room, leaning against the dresser, staring at me with a faint smile.

"Why are you marrying my best friend?" she asks. Her head tilts to the side, waiting for me to answer.

Are we really going to do this now?

"Because I love her," I say, and the words sound far more convincing that even I realize. I do love her—at least it's the early stages of love—but I'd do anything for Harper, and is that not love?

There's so much I can't tell Kensley.

Ashton throws open the door; he looks quite heated and then glares at Kensley. "You're here?"

"Of course, it's my best friend's wedding," she says and then glances at the clock behind me.

Something feels—*off*.

Ashton shuts the door behind himself quite forcefully and tears across the room at Kensley. "Where the hell is Harper?"

Her eyes wince, and she reaches forward, handing me the folded sheet of paper.

"It's not your vows," she says, grazing my hand. "But you might want to read it alone."

"You're not going anywhere," I growl, snatching the page from her grasp and quickly unfolding it.

It's definitely her handwriting. I recognize it from all the notes she took in class, which makes my heart ache even more.

Clenching my jaw, I breathe in through my nose, trying not to fall apart, because whatever letter she's giving me, it can't be good. No one writes a love letter to their partner on the day of their wedding, unless it's their vows.

And this is certainly not Harper's wedding vows.

Luca,

I'm sorry. Please forgive me for everything. I never wanted to hurt you. But I can't marry you. Not today. Not when you don't love me or Zeke. Forcing us to wed is a mistake. We both know that the only reason you agreed was to protect me. It's my turn to protect you. Please don't chase after me. Let me go. I'm setting you free.

Harper

The air rushes out of my lungs, and at least the bed is behind me as I collapse onto it, reading the letter once, twice, three times over.

"She fucking left me."

To Be Continued...

The story continues in *Between Fire and Frost* (Crimson Ice Book Three).

Fiery betrayal. Frost-bitten revenge.

A romance that was never meant to happen...

Nova has always been off-limits—Luca made that clear to every player on the roster. His little sister. His rule.

But Ashton Rinaldi doesn't seem to care ... and the spark between them is already burning out of control.

And that isn't the only secret being kept from Luca...

Liam has spent this semester buried in hockey— training harder, pushing further, determined to carve out his own future. But when Luca asks for a favor, everything changes.

Because Bristol Greyson is back.

The girl from Liam's past—the one tangled up in every mistake he swore he'd forget. And her father, Kyler Greyson, now owns the NHL's Ice Dragons.

Luca wants an introduction.

The NHL draft is looming.

But is Luca ready for the pressure...

Between fire and frost, loyalties fracture, secrets thaw, and desire threatens to consume everything in its path.

SHOP SIGNED AND EXCLUSIVE EDITIONS

THANK you so much for reading Between Ice and Oaths. I hope you enjoyed the novel. Be sure to sign up for my newsletter for up-to-date new release details, sales, early release news, and more!

If you love signed paperbacks, special edition books, book swag, or discounted book bundles be sure to check out my online bookshop: https://shopwillowfox.com

ABOUT THE AUTHOR

Willow Fox has written in multiple genres. She's written everything from young adult dystopian to spicy RomCom novels. Her books have been translated into five languages and sold across the world.

Whether Willow is writing romance or sitting outside by the bonfire reading a good book, she loves the magic of the written word.

Follow her on any of her social media sites or through her newsletter!

Willow also writes kinky romance books under the pen name Allison West.

Visit her website at:

shopwillowfox.com

Obsessive Boss

Dangerous Boss

Bossy Single Dad Series

Billionaire Grump

Mountain Grump

Bachelor Grump

Ice Dragons Hockey Romance

Faking it with the Billionaire

Daring the Hockey Player

Arresting the Hockey Player

Crimson Ice

Between Blades and Blood

Between Ice and Oaths

Between Fire and Frost

Between Sin and Silence

Between Steel and Secrets

Want more kinky romance? I also write under the pen name Allison West.

Gem Apocalypse Series

Emerald Rebellion

Amber Voyeur

Sapphire Sacrifice

Scarlet Assassin

Crimson Crown

Royally Claimed Series

Palace Secrets

Maiden Claimed

Grave Misfortune

Academy of Littles

Little Etta

Little Gigi

Little Eliza

Reforming the Rebellious

Little Lizzie's Reform (Little Lizzie)

Little Prim and Proper (Little Kat)

Virtue and Vice

A Proper Punishment (Little Lena)

Little Brides (Little Clara)

Dowries and Deception

Delia's Debt (Little Delia)

Decoy Bride (Little Vera)

Jessie's Secret

Violet's Penance

Piper's Escape

Fiery Luna

Little Jade

Little Alice

Little Love Bundle/Western Daddies

Little Samantha

Little Lexa

Little Autumn

Little Rosie

Prefer a sweeter romance with action and adventure?
Check out these titles under the name Ruth Silver.

Aberrant Series

Love Forbidden

Secrets Forbidden

Magic Forbidden

Escape Forbidden

Refuge Forbidden

Nightblood

Royal Reaper

Stolen Art